THE ADVENTURES OF THE GUARDIAN

URBAN LEGENDS

LEE WARD

FriesenPress
Suite 300 - 990 Fort St
Victoria, BC, V8V 3K2
Canada

www.friesenpress.com

First Edition — 2017

ISBN
978-1-5255-0119-7 (Hardcover)
978-1-5255-0120-3 (Paperback)
978-1-5255-0121-0 (eBook)

1. *Fiction, Science Fiction*

Distributed to the trade by The Ingram Book Company

TABLE OF CONTENTS

PROLOGUE

The Searcher knew he was badly wounded and wouldn't last much longer. The Cocoon had already enveloped him but the nanites were having trouble making repairs. Not only had he been injured in the meteor shower, The Cocoon indicated that it had been damaged. The Searcher's injuries and the repairs of The Cocoon were proving difficult for the nanites. The readout indicated that a planetary environment was necessary for the proper healing of both.

The Searcher initiated a scan, activated the protocol override, went into Hibernation Mode and switched on automatic record and flight. The readout detected a small blue planet with seven continents. The Cocoon set course for this convenient world.

. . . .

EARTH TWENTY YEARS AGO...

Ben sighed, trying to wipe sweat from his forehead and not drop the old TV camera for the hundredth time. Most normal people were in bed on sweltering July nights. He was following his uncle the former film and television star around the woods. They were chasing ghosts, goblins and most elusive of all, his uncle's former fame. He sighed again and pointed the camera at his uncle who had stopped walking for no apparent reason.

"This is Isaac Bradbury coming to you from the area known as Maiden's Bridge. We are going to capture video proof of the apparition people have seen here over the last hundred years." Isaac Bradbury said flashing his perfect and expensive smile.

"Are you sure, this is the right place? I don't see a bridge. Just trees and rocks," Ben said cautiously.

"Of course, I am. Now get a shot of the stars for dramatic effect. Hurry up, before a security goon from Eureka Industries shows up," Uncle Isaac ordered.

Ben sighed again. He'd almost forgotten that not only had he been dragged out here, they were committing a crime. Just so his uncle could film an urban legend that didn't exist. There was no point arguing so he obediently filmed the stars.

Suddenly, the view from his camera went from a clear night sky to static. The camera started making a high- pitched squeal.

"The Maiden's here!" Uncle Isaac shouted.

Ben heard a tremendous boom like thunder and was blinded by a flash of light.

Ben found himself on the ground. As he struggled to his feet he saw his uncle running deeper into the woods.

"Bring the camera! I just saw a meteor. This will make my career!" Uncle Isaac called over his shoulder.

Ben picked up his camera and followed nervously after his uncle. He listened carefully for any signs of pursuit or danger in the suddenly creepy woods. It was absolutely silent. Ben shivered.

He caught up with his uncle. The trees started to thin out and Ben could make out a clearing through his viewfinder. As they got closer Ben wasn't sure this was a clearing. He could see broken and bent bits of wood. A smell like burnt toast drifted to his nose on the breeze. They walked to the edge of the clearing and Ben saw a huge crater. A twig snapped and Ben could hear voices.

"Let's get out of here. That crater looks like a bomb went off and somebody's coming. Uncle Isaac said.

• • • • • • • • • •

Officer Mathew Rigby sat in the parking lot of Cowboy Tom's Family Feed Bag trying to eat his melting ice cream cone and look official. Being a police officer wasn't nearly as interesting as he thought two months ago. He wished something interesting would happen in this city.

• • • • • • • • • •

THE PRESENT...

A figure dashed across the rooftop. Those watching him saw what appeared to be a person wearing a suit of armour. The figure looked like someone who was dressed as a knight on his way to a costume party. However, those watching the figure knew the armour was no costume. It was in fact a highly advanced weapon. A weapon which belonged to them and that they wanted back, no matter the cost.

The residents of Braxton had named the figure The Guardian. His recent appearance had given the city the idea that heroes were not just something that existed in comic books and the movies. The city had its' own personal protector.

The Guardian's real name was Kevin Rigby. He was fifteen years old and he still couldn't believe this was happening. Was he really on his way to rescue people? Did everybody think he was some kind of superhero? All he knew for sure was that he had received a threat telling him that he must turn over his suit or hostages would suffer.

He knew he must refuse and he had to save the hostages. How had he gotten into this? The day of the field trip had started so normally. By the next day though, he'd gone from being Kevin Rigby, your average kid, to The Guardian.

CHAPTER ONE:
KNIGHTS AND ALIENS

TWO WEEKS EARLIER...

The knight charged up the hill. He could hear the screams of the damsel in distress. Reaching the top of the hill he could see where the damsel was trapped in her tower prison. Before he could reach her a dragon came swooping down out of the sky, blocking the path of the knight. Drawing his sword, the knight jumped from his horse. Confronted by the knight, the beast issued a blast of flame. Raising his sword, the brave knight prepared to slay the dragon. He swung his weapon back, ready to strike.

Kevin Rigby woke with a start causing the book he had been reading to fall to the floor. Leaning out of bed, he picked it up. He looked at the cover, which featured a knight confronting a dragon.

Kevin closed the book and jumped out of bed. He was too excited to sleep. Today was the day of the field trip to Eureka Industries, one of the top science and technology firms in the world. He was so busy daydreaming about the tour that he'd almost forgot about the English essay due that day. If he didn't hand it in he couldn't go on the field trip. Printing out a copy, he also quickly downloaded it onto his jump drive which he hung around his neck.

He always kept his jump drive around his neck because he had such bad luck with the school's computer system which was out-dated and kept crashing. Using a laptop hadn't helped his luck. Once, at the end of a test someone had bumped his desk, knocking the laptop on the floor and other times several unfortunately timed power outages had also erased Kevin's work. As a result, he was extremely careful about saving his work. He also liked writing poetry and could never know when he might be inspired.

Minutes later, he dashed into the living room, set down his cereal and turned on the TV. *The Braxton Morning News* was on and the anchor was in the middle of a report.

"Police say that this series of fires is likely the work of arsonists. They encourage anyone with information to call the department or the special tip line. And now over to Ben Simmons, standing by, outside of Eureka Industries."

A grinning reporter standing outside a tall office building appeared on screen. Standing next to him was a woman in a business suit. She was tall with black hair that had a touch of grey. Kevin was just wondering whether she could possibly be the person he thought she was when Ben Simmons answered his question.

"With me is Helen Montgomery head of Eureka Industries who is granting us a rare interview. Thank you for joining us this morning Helen," he said.

"Thank you for having me Ben. I'm glad to be here," she said with what Kevin thought was a forced smile.

"Mrs. Montgomery you've been traveling around the world for the past three years. Can you tell us anything about your travels?" Ben Simmons asked.

"I've been gathering the best scientific minds for my company from around the globe," she answered.

"Rumour has it that you're looking to take the company in a new direction. Is this true?" Ben Simmons asked with a slight smile.

"Yes, it is Ben. Of particular interest to us is increasing public education about science and technology by providing tours for schools. Through this, we hope to increase public awareness of technology issues and their practical applications. I have recently been doing important research abroad regarding the use of computers in education for children. Providing computers for schools is an important part of this program," Helen replied.

"Is it true that your company does secret research that might be dangerous to the public?" Ben Simmons asked grinning.

"I assure you, we've taken all appropriate precautions for the public. As for the top-secret research you referred to, that is nothing more than rumour mongering and internet gossip," Helen answered with a slight frown.

"Thank you for your time, Mrs. Montgomery. And now back to the studio," Ben Simmons said.

Kevin's Mom entered the living room carrying the laundry basket. She walked over to the couch and started sorting through the basket.

"Morning Mom," Kevin said.

"Good morning Kevin. I don't suppose you remembered to pack your asthma and rash medications?"

Shortly afterwards, having collected his medications Kevin was riding the school bus. He was absorbed in his book, picturing himself as usual in the role of the knight who was about to kiss the princess, when he felt someone standing over him. Looking up, he saw his best friend Will Brown.

"Dreaming of chivalry, I see, even after Mindy Carson pushed you in the mud for holding open the door," Will said.

Kevin glared. He hadn't found that very funny but Will sure did. He had only been trying to be a gentleman as chivalry demanded. Mindy had been holding a stack of textbooks and trying to talk on her cell phone. For his good manners, he found himself covered in mud and being stalked by her very large brother Travis. In fact, now that he thought about it, something he tried not to do, he needed to be careful.

“I’m sorry Kev. Don’t glare at me. You know I laugh when I’m stressed. Can I sit down?” Will asked.

“True, but I still don’t think it was funny,” Kevin said gesturing to the seat next to him.

Will sat next to Kevin and they began discussing the trip to Eureka Industries when they were interrupted by their classmate Alex Moor.

“I’m really looking forward to the tour. I wonder whether we’ll see the alien technology hidden in Eureka Industries,” he said grinning.

“What?” Kevin asked as Will simply stared.

“Sure. Didn’t you know that Eureka Industries is cannibalizing alien technology and that’s why their products are always so far ahead of other companies?” Alex said.

Kevin didn’t answer, but he thought these must be those rumours mentioned on the news.

“When did you hear this?” Will demanded.

“I read about it on *The Truth Revealed* website,” Alex answered shrugging.

“I guess we’ll find out,” Will said.

CHAPTER TWO:
THE COST OF CHIVALRY

Kevin was still lost in thought about the field trip and the things he'd heard when the bus arrived at Braxton High. Will's tap on the shoulder brought him back to reality. Kevin shook himself. Drifting off in thought at Braxton High School was a bad habit.

The building might look inviting with the benches, bicycle rack just outside the doors, the well-kept grass and the Spirit Week sign but Kevin knew better. The school contained many dangers and might as well have been the lair of some beast from one of his books. With that thought he remembered he was still being stalked by Travis Carson.

"Be careful Will, Travis is probably waiting for me," he said grabbing his friend's arm when Will stood up.

"Calm down, Kev. He can't keep this up forever. He's probably not mad anymore," Will said.

Kevin shrugged. He hoped Will was right but somehow, he didn't think so. Travis was noted for his ability to hold a grudge. Besides he was a bully dedicated to his work. He looked around but saw no sign of trouble. He started sneaking across the school yard trying to avoid notice and listening hard for telltale signs of danger. He got halfway to the entrance when he heard a shout.

"Ready or not Rigby here I come!"

Kevin spun around and saw Travis Carson heading towards him with a broad smile. Kevin made a break for it, sprinting for the entrance, but Travis blocked his path. Kevin was amazed that someone with the build, appearance and attitude of your average ogre moved so fast. Before he knew it, Travis had grabbed the back of his shirt and spun him around. There were as usual, no teachers anywhere to be seen.

"Okay Rigby. How will you be paying today's toll? Your options are your lunch and or lunch money, a pounding or a trip into the garbage," Travis said grinning.

Kevin would have answered but he was too busy searching for his inhaler and gasping. Travis laughed while waiting for Kevin to finish using his inhaler. By this time, a crowd had gathered. Travis stood basking in the attention as if he was on stage. After a suitably dramatic pause, so that he could be sure everyone was listening he turned to Kevin.

"What's your choice Rigby?" he asked.

"I'm not paying you," Kevin said.

"What did you say?" Travis snapped.

Kevin didn't answer. He was too shocked with himself. Why had he done that? Will was right. He'd been reading his books too much. He was thinking too much like he was some kind of hero. He suddenly noticed the near silence of the watching crowd. Everyone was looking at him.

"He said he's not paying you," Will said.

Kevin jumped slightly and looked around. Will was standing behind him. Kevin wondered if he was trying to make up for laughing at him by backing him up. Kevin glanced at Travis. He stood there with his mouth open slightly staring at them. The crowd of students held its breath.

"Well, it looks like the garbage for both of you," Travis said grinning.

"Nobody will be paying you anymore," Kevin said.

If Kevin hadn't so surprised by his own bravery, he might have reacted in time but before he knew it Travis had grabbed him by his shirt and dragged him over to the garbage cans. Kevin couldn't believe that he'd been so excited when he woke up this morning. He was going to spend the day smelling like garbage. Suddenly, Travis halted.

"What's on your chest?" he shouted pointing at Kevin's chest and looking revolted.

Kevin looked down at the bright red rash that had been exposed when Travis grabbed his shirt. Kevin thought fast and found sudden inspiration.

"A rash, and it's highly contagious too," he answered brightly.

Travis yelped and released Kevin. Kevin smiled. Maybe the rash wasn't such a bad thing. He walked over to Will who was also grinning. They had to hurry or they'd be late for English and maybe miss the field trip.

"Good thinking Kev," Will said clapping him on the shoulder.

"Thanks. I remembered that he has a germ phobia from kindergarten," Kevin said.

"How did you get that rash anyway?" Will asked.

"I'm allergic to Mom's new laundry detergent," Kevin said.

"What is it with you and those *Tales of Chivalry* books anyway? Look at the trouble they get you into," Will said.

"They provide an honour code to live by, and knights were the guardians of the innocent. They always rescue everyone. Beside they're fun." Kevin said.

"Whatever you say Kevin," Will said shrugging.

They made it to English just in time and handed in their essays. As usual Kevin thought of a few last-minute improvements he could have made. As he sat down in his front row desk he decided that he did worry too much. This could still be a good day. The field trip should be a blast.

Later that morning, Kevin and Will arrived at the science lab. The field trip to Eureka Industries would be that afternoon with this class. Mr. Hill waited for everyone to sit down and then surveyed the class sternly.

"Okay everyone. I've worked very hard to arrange this field trip and I expect you to be on your best behaviour. Remember that you are ambassadors of T. H. Braxton High School. This will not to be a repeat of the senior's ski trip and the cow in the swimming pool. For safety reasons, we will be using the buddy system. You're to remain with your partner at all times," he said.

"Can we pick our partners?" Alex asked.

Mr. Hill surveyed them sternly again and glanced toward Travis and some of his friends.

"The purpose of the buddy system is to break up the usual social groups of students. Oh, and no questions about aliens or UFO landings please," he said smiling slightly.

As Mr. Hill began reading his list of assigned partners, Kevin felt slightly nervous. This kind of thing never worked out well for him. His trepidation was confirmed as Mr. Hill reached his and Will's names.

"Group eight, Kevin Rigby and Travis Carson, group nine, Alex Moor and Will Brown," he read.

Kevin looked at Will and saw his unhappiness reflected on Will's face.

Once Mr. Hill had finished assigning partners he stood up and walked over to the front of the class and wrote the word 'Ethics' on the blackboard. After this he turned back to the class to address them once again.

"Since you will be seeing a top research facility this afternoon, this seems like an appropriate topic for today's class. What question should you be asking about ethics and scientific research?"

Remembering the reporter's remarks about safety concerns, Kevin raised his hand.

"Yes Kevin," Mr. Hill said nodding.

"Is your experiment safe?" Kevin said.

"That's right. This is the most important questions researchers will come across. Will the subjects of my experiment be harmed by what I'm doing? The usual response to this dilemma has a number of elements. One solution is to ensure that no permanent harm comes to participants. Most ethics codes permit temporary damage to research participants. The issue then becomes whether the benefits of research will be greater than any harm done," Mr. Hill said.

When Kevin considered Mr. Hill's comments, he found himself feeling troubled. Apparently, he wasn't the only one because Will raised his hands with a slight frown.

"Yes William?" Mr. Hill said.

"How can you know if harm happened until after the experiment?" Will said.

"You probably can't. This is the reason for the permanent damage clause. Even with this clause, there is usually a further clause that unofficially states that permanent damage can be done if absolutely necessary. The dilemma of the researchers is finding this line between ethical and unethical research. Public outcry about this line having been crossed or concern about the consequences of research more often creates ethical standards then researchers do," Mr. Hill answered.

Gathering their things at the end of class, Kevin turned to Will.

"So much for this field trip," he said and Will nodded.

Together they headed into the hall way where they saw Travis bullying a younger girl. He seemed to be inquiring about the state of his homework. Kevin headed for the pair with a purposeful stride.

"Leave her alone Travis," he said.

"What are you going to do about it Rash Boy?" Travis demanded.

Kevin smiled to himself. He knew very well that despite Travis's insult he was not about to touch him and risk catching that rash.

"You'll see," Kevin told him calmly.

"I am going to pound you Rigby," Travis snarled.

"What is going on here?" a mild voice said.

Travis looked around in shock to see Mr. Hill coming down the hall. Kevin tried not to smile. His timing had been perfect. He knew that Travis wouldn't stop to think that the break between classes applied to teachers too.

"Well, is anyone going to answer me?" Mr. Hill asked with his arms folded.

"Travis has been forcing me to do his homework and was threatening me about it being late," the girl answered.

"Thank you, Amanda. Is this true Travis?" Mr. Hill said.

"I heard him," Kevin replied.

"Travis, I can't allow you to cheat. You will do a two-thousand-word essay on what you learn at Eureka Industries. Come with me and we'll discuss it," Mr. Hill said.

Kevin watched as Mr. Hill led a protesting Travis back to the science lab. He felt a mild sense of satisfaction, though he was worried about possible payback that afternoon.

"Thank you, Kevin," Amanda said.

To Kevin's surprise she kissed him on the cheek and walked away before he could respond. He walked back to where Will was waiting, looking somewhat surprised himself.

"See. That is one of the perks of chivalry," he told Will.

Kevin smiled to himself and they headed toward the computer lab where he emptied his jump drive.

CHAPTER THREE:
EUREKA INDUSTRIES

Kevin and Will joined the other students who were going on the field trip to Eureka Industries at the school entrance. Mr. Hill was waiting with the other chaperones, clipboard in hand.

"Good afternoon everyone, we will arrive at Eureka Industries at noon. Please find your buddy now. Remember to be on your best behaviour or there will likely be no future outings for this class, or anybody else. Remember, because this trip will go beyond regular school hours your parents will be meeting you back here," he said.

Half an hour later, the bus pulled up outside of the building Kevin had seen on *The Braxton Morning News*. It was a large skyscraper with what looked like a solar system on the roof with a giant Mobius strip replacing the sun in the center, and Eureka Industries written under the logo.

To Kevin's surprise, he saw Helen Montgomery waiting for them. She had exchanged the business suit for a lab coat. As they filed off the bus she shook hands with Mr. Hill. Once everyone was off the bus she turned to address them.

"Welcome to Eureka Industries. I am Dr. Helen Montgomery. I apologize for making you miss lunch. I think I must still be on British time. Please enjoy a complimentary meal in the cafeteria," she said.

The class proceeded into the cafeteria which was full of small round tables, with a smell of fresh baking and a buzz of conversation in the air. Helen Montgomery was busy pointing out some features of the cafeteria menu when she was approached by a short stocky man.

"Excuse me Helen, Nigel wanted a word about Project Taylor," he said.

"Peter, I was just getting this tour group settled since Dr. Sharpe was running behind. I'll meet with Nigel when he arrives. It'll give me a chance to see Mike," she said, gesturing to Mr. Hill.

"Michael Hill. Come home to roost, have you?" Peter said.

"I teach high school science now. I'm just here as a chaperone today," Mr. Hill said coldly.

"Here comes Dr. Sharpe now. Come along Peter," Helen said, breaking the suddenly awkward silence. She and Peter walked away, bidding the group goodbye.

After standing in line to get lunch, Kevin and Travis found seats at a table. They were soon joined by Will and Alex. To Kevin's surprise, as he and the others started eating, Travis took a notebook out of his backpack. Kevin was about to inquire about the notebook when Will's thoughtful frown distracted him. He was staring off into space at something only he could see.

"What's up?" Kevin asked.

"I was just thinking that it sounded like Mr. Hill used to work here. If he did, why not mention it this morning? I wonder what his job was," Will said frowning.

"Maybe he was involved in back-engineering the alien technology that the company is using," Alex said, grinning and waving his spoon.

"Just because you read it on a web site doesn't mean it's true Alex. I'll bet you fifty dollars that I can prove there is no alien technology anywhere in this building. You should be careful or you'll spill your ice cream." Will said.

"It's a deal," Alex answered.

Alex reached across the table to shake hands with Will and knocked his carefully prepared sundae; vanilla ice cream, chocolate sauce, peanuts, whip cream and all into his lap.

"Oh great, I need to find a bathroom so I can at least try and look presentable," Alex muttered.

"I'll go with you. I have to apply my medication anyway," Kevin told him.

"We all have to go. We're not supposed to leave our partners," Travis said.

"Since when do you care about rules?" Kevin asked Travis, raising his eyebrows.

"I just don't want to have to do any more punishment reports," Travis said, shooting Kevin a menacing look.

Kevin decided it was best not to pursue the subject and hastily reminded them about his rash and Alex's pants. The four boys looked for Mr. Hill but he was nowhere to be seen. They did see one of the other chaperones and told her where they were going. It was only then that they realized they didn't even know where the bathroom was. They approached a janitor who was heading in their direction with a cleaning supply cart.

"Excuse me, where can we find a bathroom?" Kevin asked.

"Just head down the hall and turn left and you'll spot it," the janitor said.

"Thank you," Kevin said.

"No problem mate."

The four boys made their way to the bathroom, where Kevin, Will and Alex entered without hesitation. Travis hung back, shifting his feet with his hands in his pockets.

"What's up?" Kevin asked.

"Nothing. Just because I have to follow you around doesn't mean I'm going in with you. It's not like I want to see your disgusting rash," Travis said looking a touch green.

"Suit yourself," Kevin said.

Kevin walked into the bathroom, where he joined Will who was standing by the sink waiting for Alex. Kevin took off his jump drive which he noticed was one of the fancier ones his aunt sometimes brought from work for him. It was blue and had a removable top and the logo of the university where she was a professor. He gave it to Will.

"Look after this for me," Kevin said.

Kevin took off his shirt and began rubbing cream on the rash on his chest. He had to admit it looked terrible. At least it wasn't so itchy that he had to wear mittens anymore. Besides, it had gotten him out of trouble this morning and provided temporary bully repellent. As he finished applying his medication he saw Alex reflected in the mirror. Alex had cleaned off most of the ice cream. It looked like the chocolate stains wouldn't be easy to remove.

The three friends left the bathroom to find a still green and annoyed Travis waiting for them.

"What took you so long?" he demanded.

"We were only gone five minutes," Kevin said.

"It seemed longer," Travis snapped.

Kevin blinked in surprise. Travis stormed off in the direction of the cafeteria. Kevin exchanged confused glances with Will and Alex who both shrugged as they followed Travis. Kevin was so busy wondering why Travis was so angry that he didn't see a man coming in time to warn Will who was having another good-natured argument about aliens with Alex. Consequently, Will and the scientist who was absorbed in a stack of papers collided, sending the scientist's papers and Kevin's jump drive which Will had chosen to wear, flying.

"Sorry sir, I should have been paying more attention," Will said helping the man up.

"No problem, I should have been paying more attention as well. There are lots of distracted people around. Why another young man just stormed right past me without even saying hello. We both seem to have dropped our jump drives," the man said, handing Kevin's jump drive back to Will.

The boys helped the man pick up his papers and returned to the cafeteria, where Kevin found Travis absorbed in his notebook which he noticed was empty. Kevin tried for several minutes to make conversation but got no response. Shrugging, he took out *Tales of Chivalry*. He didn't have a chance to read however, as Will and Alex arrived.

Will handed Kevin's jump drive to him. Kevin hung the jump drive around his neck and tucked it into his shirt. Looking around he saw Mr. Hill enter the cafeteria and walk over to a young man whom he assumed was Dr. Sharpe. He had blond hair, glasses and a lab coat with the Eureka Industries logo.

After speaking briefly with Mr. Hill, Dr. Sharpe stood up, took a clipboard off the table, checked something and then spoke.

"Now that your teacher is back from the bathroom, we can get started. Everyone here for the one o'clock tour, please follow me."

Kevin and the others stood up as the class lined up behind Mr. Hill. Travis moved to stand beside Kevin. His earlier annoyance seemed to have vanished. He wore a thoughtful expression and leaned closer to Kevin as if he were going to say something and didn't want to be overheard.

"I wonder where Mr. Hill really was. Nobody came into the bathrooms when we were there. I didn't see him come out of any of them either but he got back here about the same time we did," he whispered.

"I don't know. There could be more bathrooms around here. It sounds like he worked here. Maybe he used a staff bathroom. Why are we whispering?" Kevin whispered back.

"Good question Rigby. I think Alex is making me paranoid," Travis said at his normal volume.

As the field trip progressed, Kevin began to think Alex might have a point. As Dr. Sharpe gave them the tour, the things he showed them did seem like they belonged in a science fiction movie. There were normal experiments like computer models which showed what the earth might look like in three hundred years, plants he claimed had been especially genetically engineered to be more resistant to cold and a computer with a processing system designed to allow it to pass something called the Turing Test.

In another room however, Dr. Sharpe showed them something much stranger; the largest fish tanks Kevin had ever seen. These tanks contained not only fish and other aquatic animals but what looked like large domes with plants growing inside them.

"This is what we call Operation Atlantis. What you see growing inside the domes are crops. Long-term goals of this project include studying the possibility for eventual colonization of the ocean by humans. In the short term, studies focus more on agricultural use of the Biodomes. Please feel free to look around on your own for a few minutes," he said.

As Kevin looked around, he noticed that Travis was busy taking notes. He had almost forgotten about the essay. He decided it was safest to concentrate on studying the fish tanks because Travis was in a bad mood. He spotted some tropical fish, larger examples of those in his fish tank at home. He looked for Will and Alex, wanting to point out the fish, but he couldn't find them in the large crowded room.

A few minutes later, the tour group was led to a set of red double doors marked with the Mobius strip surrounded by a large star field. Dr. Sharpe turned to the group with his arms spread out. He reminded Kevin of a ringmaster. The only thing missing was a top hat.

"This room is probably responsible for all of the rumours surrounding this company. Behind these doors is equipment used to monitor outer space for possible extraterrestrial signals," he announced into stunned silence.

"We don't expect to ever receive an answer but we figure that there is always the possibility. The more practical purpose for this room is monitoring for new asteroids, planets and comets," Dr. Sharpe said beaming.

Kevin followed the rest of the group into the room. He saw computer monitors and star charts on every surface. He thought the system must be automated because he didn't see any technicians. They were told to look around again. Kevin walked over to a monitor with what appeared to be a photograph of a star from a space telescope called

Argus. As Kevin approached the monitor, Travis trailing behind taking notes, the monitor went blank and the lights went out.

"Please remain calm. We should have the problem fixed shortly. In the meantime, I'll tell you about one of our research projects," Dr. Sharpe said.

He was using a flashlight he had found somewhere and gestured for them to gather around in the light it provided. Kevin sat down next to Travis as everyone formed a circle. Kevin was reminded of storytime in kindergarten, and was reminiscing to himself when someone whispered in his ear.

"Hey Kev," the voice whispered.

Jumping slightly, Kevin looked up and saw Will standing behind him. Alex stood next to him grinning. Kevin looked around to make sure they could not be overheard. Everyone else seemed preoccupied either with finding a place to sit or involved in their own whispered conversations. The only exception was Travis, who had already seated himself and was watching Dr. Sharpe's every move.

"Where have you been?" Kevin whispered.

"We were exploring. I have to prove there is no alien technology around here. I have a bet to win," Will said smiling.

"This room might have done that for you," Kevin said, smiling at Will's sour look as he sat down.

"Why?" demanded Alex as he settled into the circle beside Will.

Before Kevin could answer, Dr. Sharpe called for their attention as he sat in the middle of the circle with the flashlight. Kevin was reminded of sitting around a campfire and half expected to hear a ghost story. He turned to listen to Dr. Sharpe whose voice echoed in the silent room.

"One of our newest important areas of research is nanotechnology. This refers to developing technology that would allow for the construction of tiny machines on the cellular or molecular level. The benefits of nanotechnology range from medical application to the ability to break down industrial waste. The problem with nanotechnology is how to build it. There is the approach of integrating smaller technology into existing materials such as a cell or attempting to build a mechanical version of the cell itself. The person who can answer this question stands to make one of the most important breakthroughs in science.

Nanotechnology has the potential to increase a person's strength, intelligence, speed, enhance their senses and heal injuries. Arguably it could create superpowers. Most companies and scientists believe that this is the stuff of science fiction but Eureka Industries is hopeful," he said into rapt silence.

Kevin looked around the circle. He saw wistful expressions as if everyone were imagining the wonderful possibilities of nanotechnology. As Dr. Sharpe continued to speak, his description became more and more utopian. To Kevin it was clear that he saw nanotechnology as a potential cure for all of the problems of society. Kevin watched his fellow student's expressions change from wistful to greedy. These expressions made Kevin nervous. According to *Tales of Chivalry*, dragons had created the world but they also had the power to destroy it. He wondered if nanotechnology could be the same.

He was distracted from his dark thoughts by footsteps. He turned to see Mr. Hill slip into the circle and raise his hand.

"Excuse me, this is all very interesting. My morning class was discussing ethics and it occurs to me that nanotechnology could be quite dangerous. What about safety measures for something so powerful?"

"Dr. Montgomery says there is no advancement without risk," Dr Sharpe said as the lights came back on.

As the tour continued, they saw many other interesting things. There was an electron microscope, along with prototypes of a toy robot and a new computer operating system called Columbus that Dr. Sharpe told them were certain to be the next must have Christmas presents.

Kevin found all of this fascinating and couldn't wait for Christmas to come. He thought robots were cool. His favourite were robots from nineteen fifties movies and the prototypes had a retro look. Travis on the other hand didn't appear to be having any fun. He was turning green again and taking feverish notes. He suddenly grabbed Kevin's arm while his other hand shot into the air.

"I need to use a bathroom please Mr. Hill," he groaned.

"Go ahead boys but hurry up, we'll be leaving soon. In fact, meet us by the entrance," Mr. Hill said looking at Travis with mild concern.

Kevin retraced their earlier route to the bathroom, hoping they would make it in time. Travis was looking worse by the minute. To his immense relief, the bathroom came into view. He knew that it couldn't have taken very long, but his fear that Travis was going to vomit on his shoes while he was supporting him made the hallway seem like a treacherous mountain pass.

As soon as they reached the bathroom door, Travis pushed past Kevin and dashed into the nearest stall, locking the door. Kevin took out *Tales of Chivalry* and started flipping through it, trying to ignore the sounds coming from Travis's stall. He had just reached his favorite story, when he heard a thud from the inside the stall.

"Are you okay Travis?" Kevin called knocking on the stall door.

There was no answer. Kevin wondered if Travis had fainted and knocked himself out. He decided he needed to get inside the stall. He pulled on the red metal door but it was still locked. Without knowing what else to do, Kevin yanked on the door again. To his amazement, the door not only opened, it came off its hinges. A startled Travis looked up.

"Sorry Rigby, I tripped. How did you do that?" he said, staring with wide eyes at the door which was now dangling from a single hinge.

"I don't know. It must've been faulty," Kevin said in a stunned voice.

CHAPTER FOUR:
KEVIN'S FIRST LESSON

Kevin and Travis left the bathroom. They were halfway down the hallway when Kevin decided to break the awkward silence between them.

"What's in that notebook anyway?" he asked indicating Travis' backpack.

"Notes for Mr. Hill's essay. He thinks it will be character building," Travis answered glaring at Kevin.

"It's your own fault for forcing people to do your homework and bullying me," Kevin told him shrugging.

"My sister blackmailed me into bulling you," Travis mumbled.

"Mindy? Do you really expect me to believe that?" Kevin asked incredulously stopping in his tracks.

"You don't know Mindy. She may be pretty but she's like the Wife of Bath. Except instead of being beautiful on the inside and ugly on the outside, she is beautiful on the outside and ugly on the inside," Travis said glaring again.

Kevin stared in shock. He couldn't believe Travis had read Geoffrey Chaucer. Maybe he'd misjudged Travis. They had been friends when they were younger. Then again, their old friendship made the bullying even worse. Kevin also noticed that Travis didn't have an explanation for forcing Amanda to do his homework. He decided to pursue some answers.

"How is Mindy blackmailing you?" he asked.

"She has pictures of me taking a bubble bath. She said that if I didn't take your lunch money and embarrass you she'd show them to everyone at school," Travis said hanging his head.

Kevin didn't respond. Travis seemed to enjoy bullying him. He was tempted to point out that bullying people because you were being blackmailed was just as bad as someone blackmailing you. Maybe it was Travis' ashamed posture, or being reminded of their friendship. Whatever the reason Kevin couldn't bring himself to make Travis feel worse.

"I can help you with Mr. Hill's essay if you want Travis," he said.

"No thanks, I deserve punishment for what I did," Travis said looking up from examining his apparently fascinating shoes.

Kevin smiled, even though he would have helped Travis with the assignment out of his sudden burst of chivalry. He was glad Travis was taking responsibility for his actions. He also thought that Travis' bout of nausea was probably related to nervousness. When they were younger he would often complain about stomach aches before tests. This made his refusal of assistance even more remarkable and lessened his resemblance to an ogre in Kevin's mind.

They headed toward the lobby of Eureka Industries, where Mr. Hill had told them to meet the rest of the class. According to their itinerary for the field trip, the bus would be picking them up at five o'clock. Kevin checked the time and realized that they had five minutes to get there.

"We're going to be late Travis," he said indicating his watch.

"We'll have to run Rigby," Travis said.

Kevin sighed and reached for his inhaler for the second time that day. To his surprise, he caught up with Travis and wasn't out of breath when they reached the lobby. They looked around and couldn't see any sign of the rest of the class. Kevin looked at the large clock on the wall which read four forty- five.

"My watch must be fast," he groaned.

"Apparently," said Travis with a slight smile.

The two partners crossed the lobby to sit down to watch the television mounted on wall under the clock. They were treated to an episode of *The Truth Revealed*, a paranormal program which claimed to reveal knowledge hidden by mysterious secret societies. Today's topic was Bigfoot.

"What is this mysterious creature? The missing link, an alien, a giant or an undocumented primate. Whatever the case, the truth will be revealed," the anchor said in hushed tones.

"Oh give me a break. Who would watch the show?" Travis said laughing.

Kevin didn't answer, but he thought he could name at least one viewer. He figured that this show's web site was the source of Alex's alien technology theory. This suspicion was soon confirmed by the anchor.

"That's all for this week. Visit our web site for an exclusive discussion of the Braxton UFO sighting twentieth anniversary. I'm Isaac Bradbury. Join me next time for more truth revealed."

They had a few more minutes to wait. Kevin took out *Tales of Chivalry* and Travis took out his notebook, and they both started reading. Kevin had only been reading for a few seconds when someone came into the lobby. They looked up, expecting the rest of the class. Instead Kevin saw the janitor they had asked for directions earlier that day.

Kevin returned the janitor's polite nod and went back to reading as the janitor's cell phone rang. Despite Kevin's best efforts not to eavesdrop, he couldn't help overhearing what the janitor was saying in the empty lobby.

"Hello Sheila. What can I do for you?" he asked laughing.

The person on the other end of the phone said something Kevin couldn't hear. The janitor laughed again.

"You don't pay me enough to clean up after you. Don't worry, I'll take care of it Sheila," he said and left the room.

A few minutes later, the rest of the class arrived. Will and Alex came and sat down next to Kevin. Kevin noticed that Alex's pants were still stained with chocolate and now were additionally stained with what looked like ink. He turned to Will intending to ask what had happened and noticed that his shirt also had ink stains.

"What happened while I was gone?" he asked raising his eyebrows.

"We got thanked for coming, handed this stack of brochures and had to wait for Mr. Hill again. Oh, here are your pamphlets," Will said handing Kevin at least thirty blue pamphlets with the Eureka Industries logo.

"I meant the ink stain," Kevin said grinning.

"I got those when Alex and I went exploring again. The janitor we met today saw us and give me advice on how to get it out. I hope it works. If it doesn't, Mom's going to kill me. She said the shirt was too expensive and I had to beg her to buy it," Will said glumly.

Kevin wasn't sure how to respond but was rescued from the awkward moment by the arrival of the bus. He and Travis once again found themselves seated across from Will and Alex. As Kevin put his pamphlets in his backpack, he noticed that Will was grinning broadly.

"Well Alex, it looks like you owe me money! We didn't find any alien technology!" he said holding out his hand.

"What do you mean? The giant telescope we saw was obviously for communicating with their alien benefactors," Alex answered.

"Come on, Alex you can't seriously believe what some web site for conspiracy nuts says about Eureka Industries now that you've been there!" Will snapped in exasperation.

"It's also a TV show," Alex said smugly, folding his arms.

Spotting the look on Will's face, Kevin sensed danger. Thinking fast, he cleared his throat loudly, causing the other three to look up.

"So, where you guys think Mr. Hill went during the blackout?"

"What you mean Rigby? Did he go somewhere again?" Travis asked frowning.

"I heard footsteps and saw him walk into the room," Kevin answered.

"How did you see anything in there Rigby? It was pitch black," Travis demanded.

"None of you could see in there?" Kevin asked softly, looking at the others who shook their heads.

Kevin sat in confused silence. He wondered whether the others were joking with him. After all he had heard Mr. Hill's footsteps and saw him come into the room. He couldn't contemplate this mystery for long because Mr. Hill picked up the microphone at the front of the bus and called for quiet.

"I hope everyone enjoyed themselves and that those of you who are participating in next week's science fair received inspiration for your projects. Since it's Friday, have a good weekend. Finally, I wish to thank all of you for a cow free experience," he said smiling.

Fifteen minutes later, Kevin was trying to read *Tales of Chivalry* and block out Will and Alex's continued argument about sinister experiments at Eureka Industries, when the bus pulled up in front of Braxton High. As he got off the bus Will grabbed Kevin's shoulder and handed him an envelope. He glanced down at the envelope. It was a birthday invitation. He'd been waiting for this all day. He was amazed Will had lasted this long. Will had been mentioning his birthday all week and sent invitations last week.

"I already have one of these," he said laughing.

"This is a reminder invitation. I've decided to have a pool party," Will said handing Alex a second invitation.

As they walked into the school, Kevin just smiled to himself. Will wasn't an excitable person. He was the type to agonize over the simplest decision, organized the simplest things with a schedule, and he was also a cheapskate. All of this went out the window on his birthday as if this was the only time getting excitable and spontaneous activities were allowed. This made each of his birthdays stand out in Kevin's mind. Watching Will was almost like going to the movies or a carnival, which was a good thing since he wouldn't be doing any swimming.

"I'll be there, even if I can't swim. This rash won't be gone for two weeks. What's with the invitation? You could've just told me this," he pointed out.

"You're right Kev, I could have but I like making birthday invitations! See you tomorrow!" he said with a manic gleam in his eye as he ran off to deliver the rest of his invitations.

Kevin looked around and spotted his dad waiting for him at the front entrance. Standing next to him was a police officer. This wasn't an unusual sight; his father was a private detective and part-time consultant to the Braxton Police Department. It was unusual to see him consulting in public. In fact, he looked slightly annoyed to be doing it now. His arms were folded and he was whispering and was indicating that the cop should do the same. Despite this Kevin could clearly hear their conversation.

"I'm telling you they have the most to gain because of Argus," his father whispered urgently.

"You suspect that they're behind everything that happens in town, Matt. Nothing connects the fires to your nemesis. Or do you have evidence you haven't shown me," the officer demanded in what Kevin thought was a smug tone.

"Okay, don't take my advice. I'll leave the file at home in case you change your mind. I'm going out of town for a couple weeks. Excuse me, I see Kevin is waiting for me," he said striding towards Kevin.

As Kevin and his father got into the car Kevin was once again contemplating the mystery of how he could see in a dark room when no one else could. He was distracted from this line of thought by his father's voice.

"Did you learn all about the Braxton UFO?" he asked smiling.

"You mean it really exists?" Kevin said blinking in surprise.

"Sure, there was an investigation and everything. That overweight cop with the beard I was talking to was the lead investigator," he said nodding.

"They didn't mention it at all. Alex didn't talk about anything else though,"

"What did you learn?" his father asked.

"Ogres aren't so bad," Kevin answered laughing at his father's confused expression.

That night at home Kevin had a perfectly ordinary Friday night. He had supper, watched TV and played with his dog Merlin and then went to bed where he read another story from the *Tales of Chivalry*. Little did he know this would be his last ordinary Friday night.

CHAPTER FIVE:
THE BIRTHDAY PARTY

Just after waking up on Saturday, Kevin noticed the first sign that his life had changed forever. He'd fallen asleep reading again and forgotten to take off his jump drive. He got out of bed and went into the bathroom to apply his rash cream.

He took off his jump drive thinking that setting it down on sinks was turning into an unfortunate habit. He took off his shirt, opened the cream and squirted some on his hand. Only then, did he pay attention to his reflection. When he finally did he stood staring into the mirror. His rash was gone.

"That's impossible!" he blurted out, forgetting he was alone.

Kevin looked away from his reflection and down at his chest to confirm what he was seeing. Sure enough, his chest was rash free. He decided he must have misread the directions for his medicine. He picked up the tube to double check. It read:

Apply cream three times a day in affected area rubbing thoroughly. Repeat application for minimum of two weeks until rash disappears.

Kevin stood there dumbfounded for a few seconds. Then he laughed at himself for being silly. A disappearing rash wasn't exactly a mystery worthy of Alex's conspiracy theories. At least he could go swimming at Will's party.

Kevin put his shirt back on and hung his jump drive around his neck as usual. He left the bathroom and walked down the hall into the living room. His mother was doing laundry again. She looked up from folding socks with a frown. Kevin started shifting his feet. That look usually meant he'd done something wrong. He wondered what this could possibly be because he'd just gotten out of bed.

"What did I do Mom," he asked in a carefully respectful tone of voice.

"Kevin Oliver Rigby please call Will and tell him you will be attending his birthday party!" she demanded giving him her magical frown again.

"I've already told him twice," Kevin answered laughing.

Laughter was apparently a mistake. His mother's expression darkened and she brandished the socks she was holding at him.

"Will has called five times today! It's only seven thirty in the morning!" she said slightly hysterically.

Kevin not wanting a repeat of Mom's super powered guilt inducing look, immediately phoned Will. He found him fully possessed by Birthday Mania. He talked non-stop without pausing to breathe. This lasted so long that Kevin not only had to shout to make himself heard, he worried that Will would pass out. Once Kevin did manage to remind Will that he was coming, Will started talking non-stop again. Only by saying he still had to buy his gift could Kevin get off the phone.

"You got his present a long time ago. I remember taking you to that new mall," his mom said.

"You did but if I'd let him keep talking I'd have missed the party," Kevin said smiling.

"Speaking of the party, you'll have to walk to Will's or ride your bike because I'm going shopping all day. If you get home before me, your father says a police officer named Cunningham might come by to pick the file for a case he's consulting on," she said indicating a yellow file folder on the kitchen table.

Kevin spent the morning having breakfast, watching TV and reading *Tales of Chivalry*. After his mom left he decided to take his dog Merlin for a walk before going to the party.

At noon, Kevin got on his bike to ride the short distance to the Braxton Swimming Pool. He saw his neighbour Mrs. Swanson attempting to persuade her five-year old daughter into her car using the usual promises of candy. This didn't work. Carol threw herself on the ground and made herself stiff and unmovable. Kevin suspected she was holding out for a better deal. Mrs. Swanson soon confirmed this suspicion.

"I suppose you think this will get you a new doll," she said in exasperation closing the car door and moving to stand over Carol.

Kevin grinned. This was a tactic Carol sometimes used when his mother babysat. Mrs. Swanson looked around and spotted Kevin. Smiling she bent down to whisper in the still limp Carol's ear.

"Kevin can see you Carol," she said in a stage whisper.

Carol immediately stood up, looked around and waved at Kevin. Kevin waved back as Carol jumped into the front seat of the car and buckled her seat belt. As Mrs. Swanson's car turned the corner a delivery service van pulled into the Swanson's driveway and a man in blue coveralls and a baseball cap got out of the van with a small package and let himself into the house.

Kevin stared at the Swanson's front door wondering why Mrs. Swanson would leave the house if she were expecting a delivery and what kind of delivery man just let himself into a house?

Then he shook himself. Will was right. He did read too much. Mrs. Swanson had probably prearranged the delivery. It was likely something that needed to be set up that required the absence of homeowners. Will would undoubtedly remind him that the world wasn't really full of giants and dragons. Speaking of Will, Kevin realized he needed to hurry or he'd be late for Will's birthday party.

A few minutes later, Kevin arrived outside of the Braxton Swimming Pool having pedaled hard to avoid any Birthday Mania related annoyance. He hopped off his bike, parked it in the bike rack, padlocked it and dashed inside. As he entered the building he reached automatically for his inhaler only to discover he wasn't out of breath. He also found he wasn't late at all, he was fifteen minutes early.

"I really need to fix my stupid watch," he grumbled to himself as he walked over to the vending machine next to the reception desk to get a drink.

"Maybe, you just can't tell time," said a snide voice.

Kevin looked up from retrieving his root beer to see what kind of receptionist would say something like this to customers. He saw none other than Mindy Carson seated behind the desk. He blushed slightly. He wondered how anyone could possibly think she had the right disposition for reception and therefore public relations. He also wondered how he could have considered her deserving of chivalrous acts. Kevin chastised himself. According to chivalry everyone deserved them. He noticed she still looked at him with the same expression of disgust she'd had on that fateful day when he'd dared hold open the door for her. Steeling himself Kevin marched up to the desk.

"I don't think you're supposed to talk to customers like that," he said lightly, sipping his drink.

"Whatever, Kevin. You can go in and tell that freak to quit bugging me about how many other nerds are here," she said coldly.

"You need public relations lessons," Kevin said indignantly.

"Whatever," Mindy repeated and apparently deciding he wasn't worth any more of her time started filing her nails.

It took Kevin a few seconds to realize she hadn't even told him how much it would cost to get in. For all he knew one the party was free. He considered chastising her again but thought better of it, considering the results of the door incident. He gave it up as a lost cause and placed the usual entrance fee on the counter. Ignoring him completely, Mindy tossed the money into the cash register, opened a fashion magazine and disappeared behind it.

Kevin decided that being ignored meant he could go inside. Without looking at Mindy again he walked past the desk and down the hall. He bypassed the changing rooms since he had already changed into swimming shorts and a t-shirt at home, and entered the double doors leading to the actual swimming pool.

As Kevin entered the poolside area he was hit by stifling heat and the smell of chlorine. He felt hard wet concrete under his feet and heard a jumble of voices and splashing. He walked over to a deck chair with a table next to it and sat down, took off his jump drive which he had automatically hung around his neck after changing and placed it along with his birthday gift on the table. Looking around he noticed that the walls were either a combination of blue and orange or a rather boring white. As if to make up for the contrast the white walls had been plastered in colourful posters saying things like: Wear A Life Jacket and Swim Safely. Ironically the largest poster proclaimed: The Lifeguard on Duty Is Your Friend and Is Here for Your Safety.

Kevin saw a pair of water slides at both sides of the pool, a diving board at the deep end. The lifeguard chairs were all conspicuously empty. The pool itself was painted blue and grey which was peeling and showing pink underneath. There was a white strip of some kind of material that Kevin suspected was there to stop leaks. Kevin wondered how the pool had passed Will's usual Birthday Mania driven inspection.

From what he could see, there were twenty about party guests including him and not counting Will and his parents. However, it was difficult to tell because of a steady stream of new arrivals. He recognized several of them from school, including Alex. Will was of course easy to spot having already been supplied with his customary birthday crown and because he was practically skipping. Kevin smiled to himself and waved.

Will ran over to Kevin, still with a manic gleam in his eye. Will grabbed Kevin's arm and started dragging him over to a table with a large pile of birthday gifts. Kevin barely had time to snatch his own gift off the table where he had left it. He realized that it was a choice between having his arm ripped from its socket and returning for his jump drive. He concluded that allowing himself to be dragged and coming back later was the better option.

"I've got a really good haul so far. There are at least thirty people here and the party hasn't even started yet," Will said grinning broadly and gesturing at the mountain of birthday presents.

"Yeah, that's great buddy," Kevin said rubbing his newly free and numb arm.

"Hey, how come you're not wearing a party hat Kevin?" Will demanded enthusiastically.

"I just got here."

"No problem Kev," Will said producing a birthday hat out of nowhere and putting it on Kevin's head.

Early on, Kevin found the party enjoyable and uneventful. The only exceptions were being thanked very enthusiastically by Will's parents for showing up and thus causing him to finally calm down and Kevin's attempt to join the brave souls in the pool.

Kevin considered them brave souls because when he got into the pool his teeth immediately started chattering and goose bumps erupted all over his body. He did brave the water for a while because he had no desire to get out and experience the usual temperature drop that occurs when a person gets out of the swimming pool. He tried to warm up by staying near the pool's underwater lights which provided small heated patches of water but gave this up when he discovered that he could feel soft areas in the hard surface of the bottom of the pool. He was worried that his foot might go right through one of the soft spots which in the best-case scenario would cause a leak. Kevin didn't even want to think about the other possible explanations for the soft spots, so he quickly vacated the pool and returned shivering to the safety of his chair.

After a birthday supper consisting of pizza and soda Kevin returned to the table prepared to thoroughly enjoy some of Mrs. Brown's delicious chocolate ice cream cake. He found that the seat next to him was occupied by Alex who greeted him happily.

"Hi Alex. By the way have you made any bets with Will today?" Kevin asked innocently.

Alex either chose to ignore or didn't notice Kevin's needling. He looked up happily from his ice cream cake to face Kevin so quickly that Kevin was surprised it didn't wind up all over Alex's pants again.

"No, but I should. Odd things are definitely going on at Eureka Industries. One of their employees disappeared last night. Apparently, there was some kind of disturbance and the cops found signs of a break in and lots of blood," Alex answered writhing in his seat with excitement.

"Where did you find about this?" Kevin asked raising his eyebrows.

"The Truth Revealed website," Alex said nodding impressively.

Kevin's simply shrugged and returned to his cake without comment. If he had learned one thing from yesterday, it was that there was no arguing with Alex on this point. Besides, he had seen strange things at Eureka Industries. He figured a slight exaggeration of these probably accounted for Alex's conspiracy theories. He noticed that Alex wasn't dressed for swimming. He was wearing a full outfit.

"Aren't you going to swim," Kevin asked through a large mouthful of cake which he then inhaled.

"Oh, I can't swim but I came anyway. It's always worth coming for birthday cake and conversation," Alex answered happily as he thumped a coughing and spluttering Kevin on the back.

The rest of supper went by without anything particularly exciting happening. Other then Will thanking Kevin for the twelfth time for his new computer game and giving him a hug, a public display of emotion he wouldn't have been capable of without the influence of Birthday Mania.

Kevin returned to the deck chair he had sat in before the party to collect his jump drive from the table beside it. He had just picked up the jump drive and hung it around his neck, when he heard the doors leading to the pool open. He checked his watch in surprise. According to it the party should last at least another hour even if his watch was running fast.

He was surprised to discover that according to the clock on the wall his watch had the correct time even though he hadn't fixed it. He also realized the party crashers consisted of Travis Carson and a couple of trolls from one of his many sports teams.

The three guys acted for all the world like late arrivals. They walked up to the table, started eating, examined Will's presents and Kevin even heard Travis apologize to Will's parents for being late! Kevin thought it was an excellent performance. Only two things spoiled the image, a lack of birthday gifts and Will's sour expression. Kevin noticed that Will's expression went unnoticed because his parents' attention was being monopolized by the three apparently charming young men.

Will dragged a chair over to Kevin so he could sit across the table from Kevin. He sat down with a sigh and his expression looked if possible even sourer.

"You'd better put the jump drive somewhere before Travis or his cronies steal it," Will said grumpily.

Kevin decided there was no point in responding. He knew from experience that Will could sometimes be grumpy enough as an after-effect of coming down from Birthday Mania. Will's lovingly planned party being crashed was likely to make his moodiness even worse. Kevin put the jump drive in Will's new backpack.

The two friends sat in a companionable silence for a few minutes. Kevin knew Will would talk eventually. He undoubtedly needed to vent his feelings. Otherwise he wouldn't have come and sat down in the first place. They had an unspoken rule for times like this. The rule required that the upset friend always talked first. The other was to wait and provide a sympathetic ear when the time came.

As Kevin performed his waiting duty he watched Travis and the other party crashers performing cannonballs off the diving board. It was after a particularly impressive cannonball that Will finally said something. Kevin thought that this was because he'd just gotten drenched by the splash. Kevin had managed to see it coming and got out of the way just in time to avoid the wave of water.

"How did they even get in here?" Will demanded testily as he shook his freshly sopping hair out of his eyes.

"His sister Mindy probably let them in. She's working the desk remember. By the way, was I supposed to pay to get in?" Kevin said casually.

The tactic worked. As Kevin sat down, Will looked up at him with a grin and a twinkle in his eye.

"No, the rental fees my parents paid covered everything. You didn't pay anything, did you?"

Kevin didn't answer He suspected their expressions were now switched as Will was definitely grinning. Kevin felt like a giant idiot. He made a mental note to demand his money back, even if it would simply end up with him in the pool instead of the mud.

After wiping off his deck chair he sat down watching as Travis and his fellow party crashers started playing a game of catch with a large beach ball. Will watched them for a few minutes, tracking the progress of the beach ball as they threw it back and forth. He turned to Kevin and smiled.

"I'm not going to let them ruin my birthday Kev. They are not worth it," he said.

They spent the next little while cheerfully discussing the video game that Kevin had gotten Will and chatting with classmates as they walked past. As they chatted Kevin looked up and saw Alex wave and make a beeline towards them. Due to his waving Alex didn't see the beach ball which had just been thrown by one of Travis's companions. It whizzed through the air and hit Alex in the side of the head. Alex lost his balance and fell into the pool with a loud splash.

At almost the same time Alex started falling, Kevin was on his feet. As he sprinted towards Alex, dived into the pool and started swimming he had only one thought in mind. Alex couldn't swim! He didn't even notice the freezing temperature of the water this time. His only thought was getting to Alex. Clothing made this thought even more urgent.

They would act like weights as they absorbed water and Alex could easily drown. After what seemed like hours Kevin made it to Alex who luckily had managed to stay above water, and pulled him to the side of the pool where Will and a white-faced Travis helped him get Alex safely onto the side of the pool. Kevin scrambled out of the water himself.

Kevin felt tightness and a slight pain in his chest. He also noted, that he was wheezing. Before he could ask for his inhaler somebody handed it to him. After taking it he felt the asthma attack subside and looked around.

There was considerable commotion going on as people realized what had happened and came over to check on everyone. It turned out that other than being soaking wet and cold, Alex was okay and was busy accepting repeated apologies from Travis. After he'd changed into some of the clothes Will had received, he cheerfully regaled Will with yet another of his conspiracy theories.

Half an hour later, Kevin was changing his clothes. He had just put his jump drive back around his neck when he heard footsteps. He looked around and saw Travis approaching. He sat down on the bench to tie his shoe and waited.

"Lucky, you were here Rigby, that's two people you've saved in two days. No thanks to me," Travis said sitting on the bench.

"What do you mean?" Kevin asked frowning.

"Oh come on Rigby. Yesterday you broke a door to rescue me and you just jumped into a pool and pulled Alex out!" Travis snapped shaking his head.

Kevin didn't say anything. He supposed Travis was right. He hadn't thought about that. He had just acted. Something else occurred to him though and he turned to Travis.

"Why crash the party Travis?" Kevin asked.

"I was the only person in our grade and for that matter practically the entire school not invited to this thing. I'm always left out," Travis said glaring at Kevin as if it was his fault.

Kevin felt privately there was good reason for the lack of an invitation. After all, his recent life was a testimonial to Travis's bullying behaviour. However, he thought of Travis's explanation about his sister and his recent behaviour was understandable. Thanks to these insights Kevin felt a pang of sympathy.

"Will was in a great mood. Why not ask whether you could come?" Kevin asked.

"I didn't think of that," Travis said his eyes widening.

"Maybe, if you stopped to think you'd get yourself into less trouble," Kevin said pulling his shirt over his head.

"Thanks Rigby," Travis said smiling and walked away.

"Call me Kevin," Kevin said.

"See you around Rigby," Travis called over his shoulder.

Kevin finished getting dressed, walked out of the dressing room and demanded his money back from Mindy who remained hidden behind her magazine and pretended she couldn't hear him.

After several attempts to break through the feigned deafness Kevin got on his bike and rode home. When he got into the yard he didn't see any sign of his mother and figured she was still shopping. He thought he could smell smoke in the air.

Deciding that Merlin probably needed to use the bathroom, Kevin waited for the dog to stop his dance of joy, put on his leash and walked back into the yard. He still thought he could smell smoke. Soon, Kevin could not only smell smoke he thought he could hear voices. A column of thick black smoke came into view and Kevin was struck by a realization the Swanson's house was on fire!

• • • • • • • • • •

THE PRESENT...

As The Guardian ran on the rooftop he realized that his disappearing rash, the swimming pool, and the fire had all been signs that his life had changed forever after Eureka Industries. After these events, he had spent the last two weeks on a collision course with this rooftop and The Dragon.

CHAPTER SIX:
THE DAMSEL

SATURDAY TWO WEEKS AGO...

At first Kevin couldn't take in what he was seeing. Then he looked around. He didn't see any fire engines or hear any sirens indicating help was on the way. Nobody in the neighbourhood realized that something was wrong.

Kevin reached into his jacket pocket intending to use his cell phone to call for help and was horrified to discover his pocket was empty. A split second later, he remembered leaving the cell phone on his dresser after deciding he didn't need it for walking Merlin. He was still groping in his pockets when the voice of Mrs. Swanson carried to his ears from down the street.

"Somebody help me. My daughter is inside! I couldn't get her out!" she yelled desperately.

Kevin suddenly thought of the dream he'd had the night before. Mrs. Swanson's cries for help reminded him irresistibly of the princess from his dream. Without consciously deciding to, Kevin dropped Merlin's leash and ran toward the Swanson's house. All he knew was that someone needed help and that there was no time to waste.

For the second time that day Kevin did something brave, that if he had paused to think about, he probably would never have done.

Just like at the swimming pool. The only thought in Kevin's mind was getting to Carol in time. He was concentrating so hard on this idea and the potential hazards he was about to face, that as he ran he didn't hear an electronic whirring sound and series of clicks. He didn't even register Carol's mother staring at him as if she had never seen anything so bizarre.

Kevin was confused when Mrs. Swanson didn't answer him when he stopped to ask where Carol was. He attributed this to her being frightened for Carol, rather than having anything to do with him. When it became clear that she wasn't going to answer him, Kevin continued running to the house, listening with all his might. He could hear a voice coming from the second floor of the house. He was horrified to realize that thick black smoke was also pouring out the window.

Kevin burst through the front door and looked around seeing the same thick black smoke that was pouring out of the upstairs window. Somewhere in the back of his mind he registered that the smoke was very easy to see through and that he wasn't coughing. He listened carefully and could hear Carol's calls for help floating down a staircase.

"I'm coming Carol!" he yelled and raced towards the stairs.

Almost as soon as Kevin shouted the pleas for help stopped. He doubled his pace. He'd never known he could run this fast. He called Carol's name again but heard no response. Panic filled Kevin. He reached the staircase and was hit by smoke and overpowering heat. Remembering his fire safety classes, he hit the floor and started crawling but the heat was winning. As he reached the top of the landing the heat intensified. Kevin knew he wasn't going to make it to Carol in time. He could see flames now and knew he was nearing the source of the fire. He also knew from Carol's earlier calls for help that she must be somewhere near the source.

The heat and smoke were too much for him. He had failed to save the innocent. As this thought flashed through Kevin's mind several things happened at once; Kevin laughed at the ridiculous quote from

Tales of Chivalry, he realized he could see through the smoke again, and the paralyzing heat disappeared.

Kevin felt a new burst of energy and determination. He now found it easy to crawl up to the hallway and turned the corner. He saw that the hallway was in flames. His brain also registered two features of the scene. One was a doorway behind which he assumed Carol was trapped. The other simply made no sense; he could just make out the silhouette of what he thought was a Chinese Dragon.

Kevin reached the door and called Carol's name again and identified himself. He received no response. He shoved his hand into the door which was slightly open. He stared at his hand. The door should've been hot but it wasn't and it almost looked like he was wearing gloves. He decided it was a trick of smoke and light. When he opened the door, he found that he was in a bedroom. It was luckily smoke and fire free. He knew this wouldn't last because he'd opened the door and provided the fire a path inside.

Kevin looked around the room. He couldn't see anybody but he did see a large closet so he ran towards it. He yanked on the closet door just like he had on the stall door yesterday. Today it opened easily and to Kevin's relief he found Carol huddled in between some of her dresses and wrapped her in a blanket.

"Why didn't you answer me Carol?" Kevin asked as he scooped Carol into his arms.

"I thought you were the other man," she said wiping away her tears.

"Other man?" Kevin asked.

"He called me Sheila. I asked for help. He said no."

'Who are you?" She asked looking up at him and coughing as smoke rushed into the room.

Kevin wondered why Carol didn't recognize him. Then he caught sight of his reflection in Carol's open window and realized he was wearing a helmet. He wondered briefly where it had come from but also seeing the reflection of the flames and smoke, Kevin decided he would worry about the helmet later.

Even though he'd only seen it on TV and in the movies, Kevin knew there was only one thing he could do to make sure they both escaped safely.

"Carol grab my neck up and hold on tight," Kevin said trying to sound more confident then he really was.

Without thinking about the consequences of what he was going to do because if he did he would lose his nerve, Kevin jumped out of the second-storey window.

CHAPTER SEVEN:
REVELATIONS AND A CHOICE

Kevin heard the wind whistling in his ears and felt Carol sobbing against his chest. He landed on the Swanson's front lawn in a crouching position, making hardly any noise. He looked up and saw Carol's mother running across the lawn to meet him. As Kevin stood up he could hear sirens in the distance.

"It's about time," Kevin muttered to himself.

Deciding it was a good plan to get away from a burning house Kevin jogged to meet Mrs. Swanson. When they had closed the distance, she stared at Kevin and took Carol from his arms.

"I don't know who you are but thank you for rescuing my daughter. You call for help at times like these and usually nobody comes. I'm just happy to know there are heroes out there," Mrs. Swanson said beaming at him.

Kevin was confused. Why was Mrs. Swanson pretending she didn't recognize him? At first, he thought maybe she was in shock. Part of him even wondered if she was joking with him but that seemed ridiculous for such a serious situation. He was about to ask why she didn't recognize him, when he glanced down at his clothes.

It wasn't his clothing at all. Instead of his shirt, he saw what looked like red cloth over what he thought was grey metal. He reached down intending to confirm what he saw by touch only to realize he was wearing a glove made of the same material. As a final surprise, when he reached up to run his hand through his hair, which was an old nervous habit, he felt not his hair but something hard covering his head.

Kevin felt like time had stopped. He had no idea what was happening. Dimly, he remembered seeing his hand in the glove when he rescued Carol. He was clearly wearing some kind of costume. The only problem was he hadn't dressed himself in it.

The sound of the approaching sirens brought Kevin back to reality. He looked up and saw fire trucks, an ambulance and even a news van heading in their direction. Kevin had the sudden feeling he didn't want to be found here in this bizarre outfit that he wouldn't be able to explain.

Kevin crept carefully through the trees in the Swanson's yard. He slipped behind a delivery truck and down the back alley. Having absolutely no desire to appear on the evening news, he did his best to avoid the oncoming news vans. The alley was deserted and the only thing Kevin saw was an old gas station that looked abandoned. The windows were dusty and cracked and nobody was around even though there a sign declaring "OPEN 24 HOURS."

Kevin approached the window to examine his reflection. He saw that he was dressed in what looked like a complete suit of armour and a helmet with a red tunic over his chest and back. Kevin couldn't believe his eyes. Not only did he have no idea what was going on but the armour looked vaguely familiar.

Kevin berated himself. Who cared if the armour looked familiar? The real mystery was why or how he was dressed as a knight in the first place. Kevin decided he couldn't go down the street dressed like this. He reached up to take off his helmet when with an electronic whirring and a series of clicks the entire suit of armour disappeared. Kevin reflection now was wearing the clothes he'd changed into after Will's birthday party complete with his jump drive around his neck.

Kevin still had no clue what was happening. The bizarre armour had appeared out of nowhere and now it had seemingly disappeared the same way. Kevin was confused, so he did what he had done since he was little. He went home.

Kevin had gone out of his way to take roundabout route home. As a result, he was surprised to find Merlin sitting exactly where he'd dropped his leash. He was also surprised find that only fifteen minutes had passed since he heard Mrs. Swanson's cries for help. Not knowing what else to do and desiring to put off contemplating the creepy suit, Kevin took Merlin for an extra-long walk.

By the time Kevin returned, his mother was home. She looked up from unpacking her groceries as Kevin tried to sneak past her and seek refuge in his bedroom.

"How was Will's party kiddo?" she asked smiling.

"It was okay," Kevin said trying to keep his voice calm and shrug casually.

"Nothing exciting happened?"

"N-no not really it w-was p-pretty uneventful," Kevin stammered.

"Oh Kevin Oliver Rigby. Always looking before you leap and being so modest. Will's mom told me about Alex," she said shaking her head and coming over to pat Kevin fondly on the shoulder.

"Oh yeah, I forgot about that. Anyway, it was nothing special," Kevin said sighing with relief and blushing.

Kevin's mom muttered something about modesty again and went back to unpacking the rest of her shopping bags.

Kevin did his best to pretend today been uneventful and perfectly normal. He did homework, read comic books, played with Merlin and he even tried watching the news. Luckily, they didn't even mention the Swanson's; only that another fire had happened.

Kevin's imaginary ordinary day came to an abrupt end when he went to bed. He decided to read *Tales of Chivalry*. He picked up the book intending to flip to *The Witch in the Dark Wood* when he glanced at the front cover and froze in shock. Now he knew why the armour had looked familiar. Somehow, he had become dressed as the knight from the cover of *Tales of Chivalry*.

Kevin lay in bed feeling numb. He picked his jump drive from his night stand, as if hoping he could download knowledge of what was happening. It was only as Kevin held it in his palm that he realized it wasn't his jump drive.

It was the right size, it was blue, but it had no removable top only a seamless single joint that wouldn't come off and in place of the university logo was a strange hieroglyphic or rune. Kevin examined the strange device closely, turning it between his fingers. It felt smooth and a strange combination of hard and soft like it was alternating between the two as he felt it.

Where had this thing come from? Kevin didn't have a clue. As he continued his examination of the device he spotted a Mobius symbol on its cord. Feeling a sudden thrill of realization, Kevin saw himself and his friends standing in the hallway as they helped a man to his feet. Who gave something to Will.

Everything became clear to Kevin in an instant. Everything from his disappearing rash, his ability to run without his inhaler, seeing Mr. Hill in a blackout, ripping doors off their hinges, the swimming pool, rescuing Carol and his mysterious repaired watch all made perfect sense. Whatever this device was, it was responding to his body or maybe his thoughts.

Kevin felt an immediate desire to put the device back around his neck and test his new theory. The part of his mind that was meticulous about schoolwork and walking Merlin advised caution. After all, he had no idea what this thing was or what else it could do. There was a time for leaping first and looking later. This wasn't it.

Kevin decided that he needed to research this device and learn as much as possible. He started to sort through all his options in his mind. He had no doubt that he had received this object from the scientist who had bumped into Will and that his jump drive had been switched for it. The answer to his riddle had to be at Eureka Industries. He decided going there was out of the question. He thought two things were likely, the suit or whatever it was probably a secret and that he would likely be accused of stealing it. He also figured neither his pamphlets nor the company web site and other public information would help. This device was the dangerous kind of experiment mentioned by Ben Simmons.

Kevin realized his careful study had hit a dead end. He couldn't go ask Ben Simmons about any dangerous top secret projects and Helen Montgomery certainly wasn't going to tell him anything. Kevin was conflicted. He longed to solve the mystery of his strange new abilities but he didn't dare act. Suddenly, he heard Alex's voice in his head.

"Eureka Industries is cannibalizing alien technology. That's why their products are always so far ahead of other companies," it said.

Minutes later, Kevin was logged onto *The Truth Revealed* website, the source of all of Alex's conspiracy theories. After skimming through some of the headlines on the screen, Kevin started to have doubts. The headlines included things like: I Married Bigfoot, Your Mirror Is Watching You, Moon Mission Launched From Man's House, and Ice Cream Company Plots World Domination.

With growing doubt about the web site's accuracy Kevin clicked on the link for a special report on the Braxton UFO. When the video uploaded, Kevin was surprised to see Ben Simmons on the screen.

"Hi, I'm Ben Simmons. I'm glad to be back as your special correspondent. Unfortunately, you're only seeing me behind this desk because we weren't granted access to Eureka Industries or any of their secret research facilities The cover-up that started twenty years ago continues," he said flashing the same grin Kevin had seen on TV Friday morning.

Kevin sighed. He decided this was a waste of time and *The Braxton Morning News* needed to reconsider their hiring policy. He was about to close the video when a newspaper headline appeared on screen. It read: Braxton Police Receive Numerous Reports of UFO Sightings. Ben Simmons came back onto the screen.

"This headline appeared twenty years ago in newspapers all over the city and on the local news when residents reported numerous sightings of strange flashes of light in the sky on the night of July fifteenth. The story was picked up first by national and then international news sources both respectable and tabloid. The story grew more elaborate with every retelling, until the truth became obscured. Now, after painstaking research and investigative reporting of every account, the Truth will be Revealed," he said in triumph.

Kevin could tell Ben Simmons was immensely pleased with himself. He leaned back in this chair wearing the same grin he had when interviewing Helen Montgomery. He paused, obviously wanting his brilliance to sink in and then continued.

"At eight that evening, a large flash of light appeared in the sky near a Eureka Industries test site and storage facility. Minutes later, something was seen falling to the earth and many vehicles belonging to the company arrived along with the police. They were quickly sent away when Helen Montgomery arrived. Early witnesses reported that some kind of spaceship was found and removed but this was later denied by Eureka Industries, the town, and the police who, this reporter thinks, didn't want to give up the advantages the alien technology afforded them," Ben Simmons said with a final gloating smile.

Kevin was dumbfounded. He didn't know what to think. It was ridiculous. Yet here he was in possession of some kind of suit that responded to his thoughts. Could this explain where it came from?

He had definitely been given it at Eureka Industries when they bumped into an employee. He picked it up gingerly and put it around his neck. He got up turned off the lights and closed his curtains but found he could still see as if the curtains were open and the lights were on.

Kevin scrolled down on his computer screen and noticed a postscript to the video that had been added today. Kevin saw with shock that it featured a picture of the man Will had bumped into. With trepidation Kevin clicked on the link and started to read.

To his horror as Kevin read on realized he knew this story. Alex Moor had told him about it. The man's name was Nigel Hawthorne.

He'd worked at several universities but had been unable to keep his jobs because of his obsessions with UFOs and aliens.

One night his neighbours had heard a disturbance and called police. When the police had arrived not only had his house been ransacked but there was no sign of Nigel anywhere. The thing that made Kevin sit bolt upright in his chair though was the report of a dragon painted on the wall.

Kevin knew this could mean only one thing; whoever had attacked Nigel Hawthorne, was also responsible for burning down his neighbour's house and likely all the other fires around Braxton lately. He also decided it couldn't be a coincidence that Dr. Hawthorne had bumped into Will, handed over a mysterious device, and then disappeared.

Another revelation came to Kevin in a flash of understanding. Helen Montgomery had been told that someone named Nigel wanted to meet her on Friday. He concluded that all of these things were somehow connected to Eureka Industries.

It looked like Alex was right after all. Kevin made the decision not to tell anyone about his suspicions or his suit. He didn't think anyone would believe him anyway.

Although he probably had read one too many tale of chivalry, he figured the suit was his best chance to get evidence someone would believe.

A few minutes later, Kevin was in his bedroom filming himself with an old video camera. The device from Eureka Industries was hung around his neck once again.

"Hi, I am Kevin Oliver Rigby. This video documents experiments involving the technology I was given at Eureka Industries. I'm honestly not sure if I should be recording this. I want to understand what's happening but I'm worried the existence of this video will come back to haunt me," Kevin said nervously.

Suddenly, the recording light on Kevin's camera turned from green to red. Kevin heard a high-pitched whistle and an unmistakable burst of static. He frowned, walked over to the tripod and picked up the camera. He saw nothing but white static and the odd noise increased in intensity.

Kevin was confused. The camera had been working fine all day. He wondered why it would break now just when he needed it to record his observations of the device. He wished the noise would stop before it caught his mother's attention. It also hurt his ears.

Abruptly the noise stopped, the static cleared up and the camera light turned green.

Kevin was struck by a sudden idea. He walked over to his bookshelf, picking up the latest *Tales of Chivalry* book. He looked carefully at the cover; memorizing the knight's armour He closed his eyes picturing himself in the armour. He heard a series of whirs and clicks.

When he opened his eyes, he looked in the mirror on the closet door. His reflection showed the same outfit he'd seen in the gas station window.

"The technology appears to respond to telepathy. The costume should be redesigned so it is less recognizable," Kevin said continuing his notes.

A few minutes later, Kevin stood in front of his closet mirror grinning. The cloth on the armour was now green and he'd removed the feather from the helmet. A large pink plume didn't fit a modern superhero.

"Something's missing. Every hero needs a symbol," Kevin muttered.

Kevin closed his eyes and concentrated on what he wanted. According to *Tales of Chivalry* knights were guardians of the innocents. When he opened his eyes a stylized G was in the middle of his chest.

Kevin heard footsteps coming down the hall. He panicked and collapsed into his desk chair. The only thing worse he could think of besides having to explain his armour to his mom would be being seen in the ridiculous clown costume the rest of the yearbook committee had forced him to wear at the school's carnival last year.

Kevin stared at his reflection in shock. He was wearing the costume complete with the horrible rainbow wig and oversized polka dot pants. Kevin found himself, wishing he were invisible just like the first time he was dressed this way. He suddenly had no reflection. Kevin glanced at the camera and saw himself clown suit and all.

"I don't want to be invisible! I demand to be dressed in my regular clothes," Kevin snapped.

He heard more whirring and clicks. Looking back at the mirror he saw himself wearing Eureka Industries technology around his neck. He made a mental note to avoid stray thoughts.

He grinned as Merlin pushed open his bedroom door and after a quick circle lay down beside his chair.

"This could be fun buddy," Kevin said scratching Merlin's tummy.

Kevin Rigby was about to learn two lessons. Being a superhero wasn't like the comics and there was no going back from some choices.

CHAPTER EIGHT:
THE GUARDIAN

Over the next few days, the ordinary town of Braxton was forced to remember its' reputation as a strange place full of the unexplained and urban legends that fascinated conspiracy nuts, paranormal investigators and just plain weirdos. The Braxton UFO Incident, which everybody liked to pretend never happened was suddenly a hot topic of conversation.

Twenty years ago, the town had been inundated with these unwelcome weirdos just because of some funny lights in the sky. The citizens of Braxton had felt mocked and humiliated. They had all been very pleased when the oddballs from all over the world had gone away. Everybody pretended everything was absolutely ordinary, to the point where the town became nicely boring again.

Some people had been hopeful that the twentieth anniversary would go unnoticed. For the most part, with exceptions like that annoyance Ben Simmons, they had been right. To their displeasure however, over the last few days a brand new urban legend had appeared. People had been seeing a strange figure on TV, in newspapers and on the Internet. *The Truth Revealed* website and television show were having a field day showing picture after picture of a strange figure rescuing little girls from fires, saving kittens from trees, climbing buildings and even foiling robberies. Some people called the figure a menace, others a freak, some called it supernatural or an alien. A very small amount thought it was heroic. The rest of the town pretended it didn't exist since this had worked so well before.

The frequency of the figure's appearance on the news and the replays of his first rescue made it very hard to pretend the figure didn't exist. The little girl's mother also claimed in interviews that she had thanked this figure before it ran away.

Since people couldn't pretend the figure wasn't real many blamed it for the recent rash of fires. This had outraged the mother of the little girl so much she constantly appeared on TV defending him.

"My daughter Carol was trapped in a burning house for a very long time pleading for help and nobody noticed! They didn't notice my cries for help either!

I am just happy to know that someone heard and that when you need help there are people in the world who will actually save you. It's like Carol had her own personal, hero" she would say indignantly.

All this forced the residents of Braxton to admit something strange was going on. The only explanation available was the incident twenty years before, which they also had to admit, had happened. No matter what anybody thought, the question on their minds was the same. Where was the figure now?

The answer to this question would have shocked everybody. Kevin Rigby was grocery shopping.

He was also working hard to discover the identity of the arsonist. By reading his dad's file, he found that the arsonist was called The Dragon because he left different styles of dragons at each of his crimes. He usually worked for hire, and other then his calling card he left virtually no evidence behind. Despite an international manhunt, this left his identity a complete mystery. The only clue was his early fires in Australia. Kevin combed through his father's file with no luck. He was sure many of the locations were connected to Eureka Industries in some way but since so much of Braxton was, this didn't help.

Between his investigation, the increased calls for help, maintaining his normal life and keeping a secret identity, Kevin was exhausted. Not knowing how to operate the suit properly yet didn't help. This was probably why Kevin was now standing in the checkout line for the third time.

As he walked into the mall parking lot, Kevin mulled over the next step in his investigation of The Dragon. He still didn't think he should go to the police. He had no evidence. The police didn't believe his dad. Why would they suddenly believe him? He didn't dare go to Eureka Industries. His only option was to keep reading the file and see if he was missing something. He needed to unmask The Dragon and determine whether he was attacking the company or working for it.

He hadn't been helping Will enough with their science project either, even though he was using it to investigate Eureka Industries. That was one of his father's investigation rules. Always have a reason other then investigating to be somewhere.

Kevin was distracted from his thoughts as yet another cry for help rent the air somewhere across the street. He couldn't be sure, but Kevin could swear calls for help had increased since he had shown up on the news. He supposed this was logical because people now knew he was around.

Kevin looked for a secluded spot to activate the suit. He knew from attempting to film himself that it interfered with video cameras. However, he had been filmed by news crews. He wasn't going to take any chances of being discovered. That would defeat the purpose of a secret identity after all. After hiding his groceries behind some dumpsters, he activated his costume and the stealth and interference modes (or at least he hoped so), and looked around for the source of the cries for help.

The visual display in his helmet zoomed in on four people across the street in an adjacent parking lot. One person was on the ground and struggling to get up. The others were standing. Two of them were advancing on the third with some kind of weapons.

Kevin ran towards them, taking care not to be seen, dodging behind buildings even though he was pretty sure he was invisible. That was another of his dad's rules. Always be extra careful. He reached the parking lot and started creeping between cars and edged around a cleaning service van until he was behind the group. He saw that it consisted of what looked like a couple and a pair of thugs who were brandishing a knife and a bat respectively. Mr. Knife advanced on the middle-aged lady.

"Look lady, just hand over your valuables, shut up and everybody's happy. Otherwise my friend over here will have to do things to your husband," Mr. Knife said brandishing his knife at the still screaming woman.

"Actually, everybody won't be happy. In fact, I will be very unhappy," Kevin said, becoming visible and grabbing Mr. Knife from behind.

Mr. Knife struggled to free himself from Kevin's grip around his neck. The armour's strength enhancement made this pointless. Even as he shouted at Bat Boy to help him, Kevin disarmed the first thug. Kevin tossed the knife aside and turned to face Bat Boy who was standing there gaping.

"You're real," Bat Boy stammered staring at Kevin.

"Either that or you are having one bizarre dream," Kevin said smiling behind his visor.

Bat Boy stood there for a few seconds of indecision and then charged. Kevin had been expecting this so he dropped Mr. Knife and jumped. Bat Boy's swing sliced through the air where Kevin had been standing. This happened several times until the thug's face was a frustrated mask.

"Stay still freak," he snapped as Kevin dodged his blow yet again.

"Yeah right, I'm just going to let you hit me with a baseball bat," Kevin answered laughing.

This hero stuff might be exhausting and sometimes tedious Kevin thought as Bat Boy aimed for his head but at times like this, it was a blast. Kevin reached out and grabbed the baseball bat.

The woman's shout warned him just in time. Mr. Knife was back on his feet. Unable to find his knife, he was charging at Kevin with his bare hands. Kevin twisted the baseball bat as he yanked it from its owners grasp and pivoted. Bat Boy sailed through the air and landed on top of Mr. Knife. Neither one moved, they had been knocked out.

Kevin dashed over to the man on the ground who was still struggling against his ropes. He was a short stocky man who looked vaguely familiar to Kevin. He untied the man. Then smiling behind his visor again, he tied Bat Boy and Mr. Knife up with their own rope.

"Are you okay?" he asked turning to the couple.

"We are thanks to you," the strangely familiar man said.

"Who are you?" the woman asked.

"I am The Guardian," he answered.

With these words, Kevin Oliver Rigby took the last steps that would in a week lead to him running across a rooftop and becoming a legend.

CHAPTER NINE:
BALANCE

Kevin hid again and deactivated the armour with a thought. He needed to figure out a better way of doing this or he'd gain a reputation for sneaking around and being odd. This was already a problem with Will. He was annoyed by Kevin suddenly switching their Science Fair project to a UFO investigation so that they had to rush to make up for lost time. He was also mad about Kevin's frequent vanishing act.

Kevin had spent the last week trying to balance his personal life with his secret. He'd learned that this was like trying to bounce the Moon like a basketball. The problem was the Moon could crush him in an instant. He glumly walked past the cleaning service truck again and picked up his groceries. He decided he had to master his balancing act before Will stopped speaking to him.

He needed to get out of there before the media showed up. This part Kevin had mastered. The trick was not moving too quickly, not drawing attention to himself, and to blend in in case he was on film. These lessons he had learned from his dad. They were essential for private eyes. Kevin knew it was important that The Guardian was seen frequently enough to keep him on the minds of crooks and criminals but Kevin Rigby couldn't be noticed.

Kevin had hoped that a UFO project would help him figure out what he might have missed that connected his suit, the Braxton UFO,

Eureka Industries and the fires. He was sure there was a connection. So far, all the project had done was make Will steadily angrier. The fact that Kevin was now going to be late again sure wasn't going to help.

Sure enough, when Kevin's front door came into view, Will was standing there, arms folded and glaring. Kevin reflected sadly that using his suit's stealth mode would've been handy.

"You're late! Did you at least get the supplies this time?" Will demanded.

"Yes, but I had to buy groceries. It'll take me a second to find them," Kevin answered examining his shoes.

"I'm sorry I snapped at you Kev. We did switch at the last minute and I'm really stressed. You know how organized I usually am," Will said in a much softer tone.

"I know. It's my fault. I just thought it would make a better topic," Kevin answered meeting Will's eyes.

The rest of the afternoon passed by without further incident. Will's mood improved as time went on. As they were programming an animation of what witnesses to the Braxton UFO claimed to have seen, Will started chatting happily.

"I still don't know why you changed topic at the last minute but at least it's more fun than electric conductivity or figuring how plants absorb carbon dioxide."

"I'm telling you that would've been cool. See, they breathe through microscopic holes in the bottom of leaves. We could've covered them with Vaseline and proved it! I have seen it done before!" Kevin said brightly.

"Sometimes you are almost as bad as Alex, Kev." Will said shaking his head.

"You can say that but I know that my enthusiasm has helped an awful lot with your grades Will," Kevin answered.

"It's been more helpful than your other obsessions. By the way, what do you think of this Guardian? I thought he looked like a knight from one of your *Tales of Chivalry* books."

"Really? I've never noticed. There are lots of crazy fans out there," Kevin answered nervously, hoping Will hadn't noticed him nearly dropping the model he was working on.

"There hasn't been anything else on TV for over a week. How couldn't you notice? I wonder what he's doing at all those fires," Will said.

Kevin decided this was dangerous territory. He had indeed been investigating some of the more recent Dragon Fires in the hope of picking up a commonality. So far, he hadn't had any more luck then Dad or the police. He did know that except for the Swanson's, nobody had been in their home at the time of the fire. He also had a vague feeling he was missing something, something that should have been incredibly simple. However, if he started discussing it with Will, he worried he'd reveal his secret.

"We still have to complete the display. I'll put on the conclusions if you want," Kevin said quickly.

"Okay. Did I tell you that Alex keeps telling me he has some kind of proof there are alien beings in town? He says there are pictures on *The Truth Revealed* website of some creature with insect eyes, wings and that blasts fire from its hand. He keeps telling me I should give him his money because it's obviously an alien," Will said laughing.

Kevin wasn't sure how to respond. This sounded ridiculous, but then his suit obviously had something to do with Eureka Industries. Nothing about the company would surprise him anymore.

After Will left, Kevin's first inclination was to pursue his father's notes for missing clues but he reminded himself about his recent vow of balance and got to work on finishing the science project. He stayed up most of the night finishing it. His mother chastised him about leaving things to last minute and shook her head.

"I feel like I've let Will down. I want to make sure this display is extra cool," Kevin explained.

"Well I'm tired. You really need to balance work and fun Kevin. By the way the police called. They'll be sending someone to pick up your father's notes. Good night."

Kevin immediately put down the glue stick he was using and started reading his father's notes. For a while he found nothing new. Some of the fires were in Eureka Industries-owned buildings. Others were competitors' buildings, and others seemingly just people's homes.

Suddenly he realized they did have something in common. A delivery or maintenance truck was often seen nearby just before the fires. Kevin realized in horror that he had seen a delivery being made to the Swanson's. Looking at the file again, he noticed a scribbled note: *Find Argus.*

Kevin stared at the words. They seemed to mean something to him but he couldn't decide what. Stifling a yawn, he flipped the file closed. Only when the doorbell rang did he remember what his mother had said. Taking the file with him, Kevin went to answer the door. When he opened the door, he found himself staring at the bearded officer his father had argued with.

"Good evening. I am Officer Cunningham. My apologies for being so late. I believe your father left a file for me," he said smiling at Kevin, who nodded and handed him the folder.

Kevin then returned to the table and the unfinished display. He wished he could go to bed but instead he picked his glue stick. He really did need to master balance. He knew he'd regret this tomorrow.

Sure enough, he spent most of the next day trying not to fall asleep in class and the citizens of Braxton noticed that The Guardian was absent that night.

CHAPTER TEN:
THE SCIENCE FAIR

FRIDAY ONE WEEK AGO...

Kevin was exhausted. He'd spent two more sleepless nights working on his share of the science project. On top of this there'd been a definite upswing in crime and emergencies. Kevin suspected people were being either more careless, or more criminal in the hopes of earning celebrity by being rescued or foiled by The Guardian.

In the last few days, Kevin had rescued numerous cats from trees, caught three burglars, six muggers and helped countless old ladies across the street. According to the news, gang violence had spiked and then plummeted. Kevin took some comfort from this last thought, and also the fact he and Will had managed to complete their display and computer animation that he was now carrying.

Kevin wasn't comforted by the sudden muggings and continuing arsons. He still couldn't figure out how they were connected to Eureka Industries. He also noticed the muggings seem to mysteriously happen after people realized that he was patrolling the area. He had only one clue; a truck from Mr. Soapy's Cleaning Service was often somewhere nearby.

Mr. Soapy and his trucks were important. As far as Kevin could find there was no such business in Braxton and there never had been.

He was positive finding Mr. Soapy would not only resolve the crime spike, but reveal the identity of the mysterious Dragon. Not that his certainty was getting him anywhere he thought, as he glanced glumly around the school yard. The vans always disappeared before he could catch them.

Suddenly Kevin spotted a van with a big pink soap bubble, wearing a hat on the side. Kevin almost dropped the display he'd worked so carefully on. That was definitely one of the disappearing vans. He immediately felt his shoulders tense. Something bad was going to happen.

He dug around in his backpack and removed a thin gold chain with what looked like a pendant about the size of a pen or eraser. The pendant had a strange symbol on it that was a cross between a hieroglyphic and a rune. Kevin recently figured out that it was actually possible to manipulate the armour's appearance in compact mode. The default still looked like his jump drive without the top. The necklace would be less conspicuous.

Kevin glanced nervously at the Mr. Soapy truck. If he was right, remaining inconspicuous today was going to be a big problem. As he got closer to the front doors he tripped and then heard a voice.

"I'm telling you Sheila. It's not smart for you to be here. You need deniability. When the party starts, you'll have to throw another shrimp on the barbie because he'll be here."

Kevin spun around and nearly dropped his meticulously prepared model and display. Luckily, someone grabbed it just as it slipped out of his grasp.

"Thanks Alex I probably would have cried and Will would've killed me," Kevin said through a yawn.

Alex helped Kevin carry the display inside and down the hall. Kevin looked around cautiously. The voice he'd heard was familiar for some reason. He was so distracted he bumped into one of the school custodians and almost smashed his display again.

"I'm sorry I'm just really nervous today," Kevin said to the man in blue overalls.

"No problem mate. I always wonder why nobody does projects about the Cane Toad. They're right pests where I come from. There's good money getting rid of them," the janitor said pushing his cart out of their way.

They entered the gym, walked over to Will and started setting up their projects Alex took a closer look at the model he was holding for Kevin.

"The Braxton UFO. Wish I'd thought of it. I guess I'll just have to settle for Medusa and the Cyclops," he said indicating his Bristol board, as Will stood with his mouth hanging open.

Kevin burst out laughing, subsiding into a giggling fit at the look on Will's face. Kevin looked over at Alex's display and read the topic: *Do Mythical Greek Monsters Exist?*

"How can mythical monsters possibly be a topic for a science project? They are mythical!" Will demanded indignantly, while Kevin's giggles reached new intensity.

"Elephant skulls could have inspired the Cyclops, and peacocks Argus and his thousand eyes!" Alex said heatedly.

"How do elephant skulls explain the Cyclops?" Will demanded.

Exactly how elephant's skulls explained Cyclops, Kevin never found out because he suddenly remembered where he'd seen the name Argus; on a picture of the space telescope at Eureka Industries.

Kevin didn't have time to contemplate this however, as Mr. Hill called for everyone's attention.

"Good afternoon, I know you've all worked very hard on your projects. And I'm thrilled to welcome a special guest judge," he said, looking anything but thrilled as Helen Montgomery walked into the gym.

Kevin hoped nobody saw him flinch and he managed to keep his face straight. He quickly stuffed the necklace into his shirt, making sure the pendant shaped suit wasn't visible. It probably would've been smarter to take it off but he didn't dare. If any of his theories were right, something very bad was going to happen. All the key players were in the school. He and Helen Montgomery were in the gym. Where was The Dragon?

Kevin's anxiety increased as time went on. Helen Montgomery behaved in a perfectly normal way. She seemed genuinely interested in everyone's projects and promised free computers for the school. When she came to Alex's project, she smiled broadly.

"Well, this is certainly a more interesting topic then the usual baking soda volcanoes. And it looks like an interesting theme is going to continue," she said moving over to examine Kevin and Will's project.

Kevin answered her questions automatically. Feeling tenser by the minute, he wondered what she was doing here. Was she a victim or a mastermind? As she smiled at them, Kevin was tempted to go with mastermind.

"I'm always fascinated by such things. Unidentified Flying Objects could mean so many things. All we really know is that witnesses saw something in the sky that they didn't understand. Did they see what they thought they saw? Did they even see anything at all?" she said smiling broadly at both of them.

As she moved on, Kevin sighed with relief. He wondered if she knew his secret. As time ran on Kevin found himself calming down. The judging portion was almost done and nothing had happened. Maybe he'd been wrong after all. That was when the fire alarm went off and smoke poured into the gym.

CHAPTER ELEVEN: THE DRAGON'S ULTIMATUM

At first nobody realized exactly what was happening. Then people started looking up at the smoke. As it got thicker and thicker, confused and panicked voices joined the blaring fire alarm.

Under cover of the general upheaval, nobody noticed Kevin's safety goggles darken with a flickering green light. He was using them as a combination digital readout and night vision goggles. He couldn't see any unusual sources of heat or any other indicators of flame nearby; just increasingly dense smoke.

"Everyone please remain calm and proceed out of the gym doors in an orderly fashion. Follow me and stay close!" Mr. Hill called calmly over the racket.

Kevin faced a moment of indecision. Should he follow the others or pursue The Dragon. Something about this didn't seem right. Braxton High had nothing to do with Eureka Industries. This wasn't part of The Dragon's pattern. Kevin concluded there was only one reason for a change. This was a trap meant for him.

Will grabbed Kevin's arm and started dragging him towards the gym doors as acrid smoke continued to pour from an overhead vent.

"Come on Kev we've got to get out of here!" Will shouted.

Kevin still couldn't decide what to do, so he let himself be dragged. If this was a trap he wasn't going to walk right into it. As the boys reached the hallway the smoke intensified so that Kevin was forced to drop to his knees beside Will and crawl. He noticed that Will was coughing but he wasn't. He also found that, like when he'd rescued Carol he could easily see through the smoke.

Kevin suddenly noticed the mural that had been added to those already lining the hallway walls. He knew no student had made this one. It depicted a large green European Dragon. He realized that the dragon was captioned with the words:

Come out come out, wherever you are.

Kevin gazed, transfixed at this sentence. The Dragon had broken his pattern because he was hunting. All this time they had been hunting each other. The Guardian had been trying to identify The Dragon, and The Dragon had won the game.

The next move belonged to Kevin. The trouble was that Kevin wasn't sure of the rules or what move to make. He still didn't see any sign of flames or feel any heat. There was only the steadily increasing smoke.

All of this went through Kevin's mind in a few seconds as he crawled behind Will and Alex. He'd just made up his mind not to fall for an obvious ruse, when shouts for help reached his ears. They were coming from the direction of the science labs, and Kevin immediately thought of Carol. This settled the matter for him. Trap or not, The Guardian was coming.

Kevin let the others move ahead of him until he was last in line of everybody who had been in the gym. He activated his armour with a thought and stood up. He looked around carefully, hoping nobody had seen his transformation. He headed in the direction of the science labs.

The closer The Guardian got to the cries, the thicker the smoke grew. Finally, he made it to the lab where a week ago Mr. Hill had discussed a field trip and ethics. *Had it only been a week?* he wondered.

The cries for help intensified as The Guardian came to a small sign which read:

Come in please.

And then for the third time, The Guardian found his way blocked by a locked door behind which was a person in trouble.

He wrenched it open. This time he did it without hesitation and without ripping off the hinges which he thought was progress. He had a feeling things wouldn't go so well when he got into the room.

"Like the sign says mate, please come in," a vaguely familiar voice said.

The Guardian stepped into the room, looking around cautiously at a number of the classroom's interesting features. There was something on Mr. Hill's desk that was presumably some sort of smoke machine as smoke was pouring out of it in into the room's air vents. Travis and one of his friends were tied up in the corner, but the strangest thing about the classroom was The Dragon himself.

It looked to The Guardian like *The Truth Revealed* website did get something right occasionally. The Dragon did look very much like an alien. He had on what looked like an old fashioned flying ace helmet that was complete with flight goggles, giving his eyes an eerie insectoid appearance, and also seemed to be wearing what might have been a jet pack.

He was sitting at Mr. Hill's desk with his feet up. Once The Guardian was in the room, he switched off the smoke machine and smiled.

"Now that you're here I won't need that. These however, stay," he said gesturing towards the boys in the corner.

"I knew cries for help would bring you. Heroic types can't resist people in trouble although I find rescuing bad for business," The Dragon said grinning and gesturing again at the struggling and obviously terrified teenagers.

"Let them go!" The Guardian demanded, taking a step forward towards The Dragon.

"I don't think so Doc. These two twits are my guarantee that you stay nice and polite during this little meeting," The Dragon said casually as he reached for a remote control on Mr. Hill's desk.

He pressed a button on the remote control and a fire erupted in a garbage can sitting in front of the boys. The Guardian dashed across the room. Before he reached the garbage can the fire went out. The dragon smiled again as he set down the remote.

"Relax mate. We have a business proposal to discuss. Nobody needs to cork it so long as you play nice. We've even got snacks," The Dragon said, picking an apple up off Mr. Hill's desk and taking a bite.

The Guardian carefully considered his next move. He assumed that the phrase "cork it" meant die. The Dragon was giving him plenty of new information. The last piece of the puzzle clicked into place. He knew he had the advantage. The Dragon didn't know his identity. His father had always told him to keep suspects off of their game plan.

"How is Sheila, Mr. Soapy?" The Guardian asked lightly, watching The Dragon carefully.

The Dragon smiled and took another bite of his apple. He cast an amused glance at Travis and his wide-eyed friend. He was taking his time before answering.

"Well it seems we've been keeping an eye on each other. I've been watching you, setting up a series of tests for my employer. I'm impressed and I've been told to offer you a business deal. Please, sit down," he said indicating the chair in front of the teacher's desk.

"I'm not interested in any business with you! You burn down houses with children inside!" The Guardian snapped.

"You do investigate properly, Michael. If you know I like to set fires; then just think of all the school children here. I've rigged all the Bunsen burners for a big show unless you talk business. I don't like hurting people. Please don't make me. We have lots of time to talk since the fire department's so very busy," The Dragon said softly, causing flames to appear at the tips of his gloved fingers.

"What do you want?" The Guardian asked, sitting in the chair.

"Your suit is impressive, but it doesn't belong to you. You're just part of a long line of thieves. My employer wants it back. You'll be paid handsomely and may even continue the superhero gig if you wish. All you have to do is hand the suit over for research. You can even participate," The Dragon said like he was reading a prepared statement.

"I don't want to end up missing, leaving only my blood behind. So, on that note, never. I am going to find out who you are and stop you mate," The Guardian said calmly.

"Then my employer says the city will burn. Fire is a beautiful thing. It creates and destroys. What I do with it doesn't matter to me. It's all business. The circumstances of our next meeting are up to you. Just to show I'm serious I'll start with these two."

The Dragon pushed the button on his remote. The fire again started in the garbage can, trapping Travis and his friend who started struggling against the ropes in a blind panic.

The Guardian had launched himself across the desk to grab the remote. He changed direction at the last minute and headed for the two boys. He grabbed the ropes, snapping them with ease. The Guardian pushed the two boys to the door. He was about to turn back to dispose of the garbage can and saw The Dragon flying out a smashed window. It *was* a jet pack.

To The Guardian's relief, the sprinklers came on a few seconds later. He turned to find Travis staring at him.

"You do exist."

"What a day! First, I am kidnapped by a guy who sounds like the janitor from the evil field trip. He spends the whole time yammering about Cane Toads, tries to roast me, and I get rescued by a superhero. I knew I should have stayed home," Travis said sighing.

A few minutes later, Kevin was standing next to Will watching firemen spray water on the flames coming out of the science lab window. Luckily, he'd managed to make it outside just after everybody else. He was confused about why nobody had come looking for him after the first head count. He had his suspicions though.

Kevin knew Alex was right. Mr. Hill had worked at Eureka Industries on alien technology. The Dragon had assumed that Mr. Hill was The Guardian. Kevin however, knew exactly who The Dragon was. He needed to confirm his suspicions. He would talk to Mr. Hill and go to Eureka Industries.

Kevin had been wrong. The bad guys didn't have the advantage he did. He was going to sweep the board and slay The Dragon.

CHAPTER TWELVE: CONVERSATIONS

Kevin spent the next couple of days planning his Eureka Industries break-in. He decided that regardless of The Dragon's connection to the company, it was where he would find answers. He'd been right about his pamphlets being no help. They contained basic public relations information which of course, included no information about his suit.

He planned to talk to Mr. Hill as The Guardian to confirm his leads and suspicions. His dad would say doing otherwise was allowing the suspect to dictate Kevin's investigation.

Before talking to Mr. Hill, Kevin wanted to confirm his theory about The Dragon by talking with someone else. This was why Kevin was making a very long distance phone call.

"G'day mate. You've reached the University of Melbourne reception desk. How may I help you today?" said a chipper voice on the other end of the line.

"Hello. May I speak with Professor Leona Rigby please?" Kevin asked trying not to laugh at the odd mixture of formality and casualness used by the secretary.

"I'll put you through. Whom shall I say is calling?' The secretary asked.

"Tell her it's Ollie," Kevin said.

Kevin knew his aunt would answer quicker by hearing his middle name because she was the only person who ever called him Oliver, let alone shortening it to Ollie. After a few minutes of being treated to elevator music, Kevin heard his aunt's voice.

"Well hello Ollie! Long time no see. What can I do for you?" she said happily.

"Hi. I'm doing a Social Studies report on Australia. I have a few questions I was hoping you could help me with," Kevin said having decided it was best to keep things simple and avoid arousing any listener's suspicions.

"Fire away Ollie," Aunt Leona said brightly.

"Okay, what does the phrase cork it mean?" Kevin asked.

"What kind of a report is this? It means die or to expire," she said laughing.

"I'm just adding some colour with a discussion of local slang.

Next question. What can you tell me about Cane Toads?" Kevin asked as casually as he could.

"Let me see they are not native to Australia. Like a lot of animals, they were introduced by settlers and became feral. In this case, they were originally intended to control a feral insect. Instead they ignored the beetle, ate local frogs, and spread like wildfire. To make matters worse, they're so poisonous they regularly kill and cause health problems for animals, the elderly and children," she said darkly.

"What did they do about that?" Kevin asked amazed, even though he thought he knew the answer.

Kevin was tense while he waited for Aunt Leona's answer. Her answer was the real reason he'd phoned. If he was right she was going to confirm the identity of The Dragon.

"The government put a bounty on the toads, paying people to kill them. You can even buy Cane Toad wallets and key chains. Put together they make up a large portion of some small communities' economies," Aunt Leona said laughing.

"What does crikey mean?" Kevin asked with mounting excitement.

"It means wow. If you saw a beautiful young lady Oliver, you'd call her a beautiful Sheila and say crikey," she explained laughing again.

"I think that's everything. Thanks Auntie. Goodbye and I love you," Kevin said trying to conceal his elation.

"Bye Oliver. Love you and come visit me soon," she answered.

Kevin hung up the phone. He now knew who The Dragon was. He'd seen him disguised as a janitor twice. This also explained the Mr. Soapy trucks. The cleaning and delivery service was a cover. Soon, Kevin would know the connection to Eureka Industries. There was still the possibility the company was being sabotaged.

There was a knock on the front door. Kevin answered it and Will skipped inside. His eyes were alight with residual Birthday Mania.

"Hey Kev, look at these," Will said excitedly handing Kevin an envelope.

Kevin looked down at the envelope. It was from a twenty-four-hour photo developer and contained pictures from Will's birthday.

"I still don't understand why you don't use a digital camera for your so-called official photos," Kevin told Will as they sat down at the kitchen table.

"Digital cameras don't have the same quality or personal touch as film. Just like film isn't the same as a portrait. Besides, mom and dad wouldn't hire a painter for some reason."

"Speaking of photography, I hear that new mall has a great photography store. The grand opening is on Friday. Want to come with me? They also have a huge movie theatre," Will said.

"Okay. We haven't hung out lately," Kevin answered grinning while hoping The Guardian wouldn't interfere with his relaxation.

They spent the next few hours going through the pictures. The photographer had captured virtually every moment of the party including the cake cutting, present opening, Alex sneezing and Will getting splashed by Travis and company. Kevin noticed that there were multiple shots of everybody by the pool after Alex had fallen in. There were even close-ups of Alex, Kevin and Will sitting wrapped in towels just after they'd gotten out.

After looking at the pictures, they played the video game Kevin had given Will for his birthday. They did fairly well until the Cyclops caught them trying to escape by lying down under his sheep. After that they played a board game. This was something they only did together or occasionally with Alex, since none of their other friends saw the point on a game that wasn't interactive. Then they watched an old science fiction movie called *Attack of the Brains from Outer Space*. Kevin had such good time he stopped thinking about Eureka Industries and The Dragon for the first time since the field trip.

Later that night, after his mother had gone to bridge club, Kevin decided it was time for a chat with Mr. Hill so The Guardian was currently sneaking around a perfectly ordinary suburban street just after dark. The street was so ordinary that The Guardian wondered if he'd made a mistake.

It seemed absurd that anyone who had any knowledge of extraterrestrial technology could live here. The street was full of literal examples of the stereotypical house with a white picket fence. Across the river, the mansions of the city's rich and famous were just visible. Or at least what passed for rich and famous in town, which mainly consisted of the Braxton family and of course, Helen Montgomery.

The further The Guardian went down the street, flitting from shadow to shadow, the sillier he felt. He could see Mr. Hill's house now. Not only did it look normal and peaceful, it looked boring. The Guardian wondered whether Mr. Hill had bought the house because it was the most uninteresting one he could find. The lawn and flower beds looked absolutely perfect. The paint was fresh.

The Guardian approached the house cautiously. At first, he thought nobody was home because all the lights were off.

As he got closer he could hear thumps and bangs coming from what he thought must be a bedroom on the second floor. He decided it was best to scale the roof.

As the news media would attest, The Guardian did like to climb things. It was odd, The Guardian thought, that he was climbing on roofs. As Kevin Rigby, he wouldn't have dared. Maybe it had something to do with his first rescue which had forced him to jump out a window, but he felt at home.

The Guardian felt Mr. Hill probably wouldn't be willing to talk to him. Hopefully, arriving through the window would be a dramatic enough to get his attention and startle the secrets of Eureka Industries out of him.

Soon, The Guardian could tell that the thumps and bangs he'd heard were being made by a frantically packing Mr. Hill. The bedroom was full of boxes and suitcases and clothing, and other items were heaped on the stripped bed. Mr. Hill was rushing around the room knocking things over. The window was open with a clear path towards it as if Mr. Hill needed a quick getaway route.

"Are you going somewhere Doctor?" Kevin asked slipping through the window.

Mr. Hill spun around, pointing a gun at the fifteen-year-old would-be superhero Kevin Rigby.

CHAPTER THIRTEEN:
MR. HILL'S VISITORS

"Who are you? Tell me! I swear I'll shoot you!" Michael Hill screamed waving his gun.

The Guardian froze. Despite everything he'd done since the field trip, right now he was a teenager whose science teacher was pointing a gun at his head. He didn't know if Mr. Hill would fire or even if the suit would protect him.

The only other time he'd faced guns had been in the hands of gang members. On those occasions, he'd done his best to avoid getting shot. Thanks to his enhanced physical agility he'd succeeded. He didn't know if he could do this today, with the gun pointed directly at his head. He could see that Mr. Hill's hand was shaking and his left eye was twitching. He decided his only hope was to talk him down.

"Put the gun down Doctor, before you do something you'll regret," The Guardian said, hoping he sounded braver than he felt.

Mr. Hill's response was scary. He started laughing hysterically, his eyes bulging, and his hands shook worse than ever.

"I don't think so. I know what's happened to everybody else involved with your device. I lower this gun and I either disappear or die. I suppose I would just become a washed up freak show in everybody's eyes. Step away from the window and give me the device!" Mr. Hill said again.

The Guardian knew two things. He was right. Mr. Hill did have information, and despite being afraid he wanted the suit. The Guardian could see the longing in his eyes.

"I am not going to hurt you. You must've seen what I've been doing with this outfit. I just want information about Eureka industries," The Guardian said trying to make his voice as soothing as possible.

Mr. Hill frowned. After a minute or two he lowered his gun. He considered The Guardian carefully. Then he suddenly ran to his bed and again started throwing his belongings haphazardly into his suitcase. Some of the items fell to the floor and smashed. Mr. Hill either didn't notice or didn't care. He kept dashing around the room, throwing things into boxes, and shooting apparently terrified glances at the windows and the door.

"I suppose you're not the assassin after all. He's been careful and crafty. You've done nothing but draw attention to yourself. It's stupid. All the rescues and crime fighting is stupid. There are people who want the device. People who will kill to get it back. In fact, most people involved with the device have died, including its original owner. I was there," Mr. Hill said with a haunted look in his eyes.

Mr. Hill resumed packing. He shifted a stack of shirts from on top of a neatly wrapped parcel. He looked around at the windows and doors again.

"Tell me about Eureka Industries. Could I get inside without anyone noticing? I need to figure out their connection to the arsons," The Guardian said, holding his breath behind his visor.

"I don't know anything about the arsons. As for Eureka Industries, I can only tell you to stay away from the place. When I worked there, Helen's father was obsessed with finding alien technology. The Braxton UFO urban legend has truth to it. I don't want to give you any more information. It isn't safe." Mr. Hill said with a faraway look in his eye.

"Why aren't you safe?" The Guardian demanded.

"Several people I worked with disappeared; Martha Collins, Eli Donaldson and now, Nigel Hawthorne. I'll be next and so will you if you keep up with the TV antics," Mr. Hill said frantically.

He continued to pack with mounting urgency and increasingly panicked behaviour. The Guardian decided to leave. Deciding that Mr. Hill's story had to be either crazy or true, he walked back to the window. The only way he'd know for sure was to check out Eureka Industries. He stopped with one leg on the windowsill when Mr. Hill spoke.

"That's funny I don't remember ordering anything from Mr. Soapy's Cleaning service," Mr. Hill mumbled as he bent over the brown package The Guardian had noticed earlier.

The Guardian jumped from the window sill. He ran to the bed and pulled the package out of Mr. Hill's hands. Sure enough, he saw the large pink soap bubble, with a big grin and wearing a baseball cap.

"We need to leave now! The assassin you're worried about sent you that!" The Guardian said urgently indicating the innocent looking package.

Mr. Hill just stared at The Guardian, his eyes wide. Despite his frantic packing, he now seemed unable to move.

"Go! I'll deal with this!" The Guardian said grabbing the package and shoving Mr. Hill towards the door.

The Guardian headed for the window again while thinking about how sick he was getting of jumping out of them. He hoped the idea he had just had would work.

As he reached the window, he looked down and saw two police officers standing at the front door. He felt a wave of relief. The cavalry had arrived but even as he thought this, he felt uneasy. The cops had arrived in an unmarked car. This might explain why The Guardian hadn't heard any sirens. If the police were here about the bomb, The Guardian realized it would be treated as an emergency. There would have been more than one car. It certainly wouldn't have been unmarked, and the bomb squad would be there as well. This led him to the conclusion that these men weren't the police.

There was a loud knock on the front door. Mr. Hill moved towards the bedroom door. The Guardian grabbed his arm, holding up his hand and shaking his head. He hoped Mr. Hill would get the message and wait. Mr. Hill gasped as The Guardian suddenly disappeared.

The armour's newly activated stealth mode allowed The Guardian to creep out of the house. He was sneaking up behind the so-called police when they called out.

"Open up this door now! It's the police. You may have received a suspicious package!" one of the so-called police bellowed.

The Guardian couldn't help feeling admiration for The Dragon. It was clever to send a package and then send henchmen to help your victim. He knew that they were henchmen because he recognized the voice that was demanding entry as Mr. Knife.

"Hello again. I thought you'd be in jail by now. Of course, you now will be for impersonating the cops. Maybe I should give you the chance to go away now and forget it," The Guardian said pleasantly.

The two goons spun around. The Guardian tried not to laugh. The henchmen stood there with their mouths hanging open. Mr. Knife trained his gun on the superhero.

"Hit the detonator. I'll take care of this freak. The package will take care of the boss's target," Mr. Knife ordered Bat Boy and tossed him a remote like the one The Dragon had used in the science lab.

"Yes please, feel free to hit the detonator," The Guardian said brightly throwing the package at Mr. Knife.

The thug dropped his gun and caught the package in his outstretched hand. He looked around in horror as Bat Boy's finger descended on his remote trigger.

"Stop! You'll kill me!" Mr. Knife screamed.

The Guardian took advantage of this distraction to tackle the terrified Mr. Knife. The package flew through the air. Everyone turned to watch as it hit the ground and smashed.

"You're crazy!" Mr. Knife said just before The Guardian punched him and knocked him out.

The Guardian breathed a sigh of relief. He'd been right in thinking he'd deactivated the bomb while in stealth mode. At least he was pretty sure he'd succeeded, since he was still alive. He turned to deal with Bat Boy who snarled and ran towards him but before he reached him there was a pair of thuds and Bat Boy hit the ground. Mr. Hill stood over the henchman with a bat.

"I figured I owe you one. Is there anything else you want?" he said calmly dropping the bat.

"If you want to feel safe again, tell me how to get into Eureka Industries." The Guardian answered.

"I don't need to tell you much. The device will show you what you need. I can tell you your answers are there. I also know they'll have doubled security after Nigel disappeared. I'm still telling you not to go there.

If anyone is demanding your suit, don't give it to them. It's too dangerous I can see now that you have the ability to look after it. You'll use it better than we did."

• • • • • • • • • •

THE PRESENT...

As The Guardian raced across the rooftop he knew Mr. Hill had been right. He probably shouldn't have gone to Eureka Industries. He knew that The Dragon and his employer couldn't have his armour. As for doing better, that depended on whether he got anyone out of this alive.

CHAPTER FOURTEEN:
INTO THE DRAGON'S DEN

WEDNESDAY TWO DAYS AGO...

Kevin planned the break-in to Eureka Industries meticulously. He knew The Dragon wanted him to go. He couldn't do it on The Dragon's terms. It was obviously a trap. Mr. Hill was right about one thing; The Dragon couldn't be allowed to possess Kevin's suit. Kevin was becoming more aware of the suit's power, and in the wrong hands it would be incredibly dangerous. He did sometimes ask himself whether his hands were the right ones.

Since The Dragon's threat, arsons were becoming an almost daily occurrence. The Guardian, the police and the fire department could barely keep up. There wasn't any pattern. Kevin knew The Dragon and Sheila were trying to draw him out.

As alarming as Kevin found the fires, they showed him why he couldn't give up his suit. He reasoned that if his enemies were willing to do these things to get it, once they had it, the things they would do would be hideous. They might even be the same if Braxton was attacked by a real dragon.

Kevin had waited until today because it was a day off school and his absence was likely to go unnoticed. His mother would be at work and his dad was still out of town. At first, he'd intended to infiltrate Eureka

Industries by night. After thinking about it though, Kevin realized that doing so during the day provided camouflage and safety. Even if The Guardian was discovered, with witnesses around his enemies would be less likely to attack.

As he approached the Eureka Industries skyscraper, The Guardian activated his armour's interference mode. He walked in through the front doors and followed a tour group going toward the cafeteria. Once inside, he pulled his cap lower. The only part of his current disguise he was worried about was wearing sunglasses on a cloudy October day.

He looked around at the tourists he was blending in with and his worries disappeared. They were the kind of people who followed *The Truth Revealed.* They were a mixture of Goths, computer nerds, and the extremely pale. One guy even had his head wrapped in tinfoil. The Guardian was definitely the least conspicuous of this bunch.

Once the group reached the cafeteria, The Guardian detached himself and retraced his route to the bathroom. Once inside, he made sure he was alone. He noticed that the bathroom stall door still dangled from one hinge. After checking all of the stalls, he activated the armour and the stealth mode. He heard the now familiar whirring and clicking that meant the armour was active. He moved in front of the mirror and saw no reflection. The Guardian left the bathroom. It was time for answers.

He needed to access the Eureka Industries mainframe. For this he needed an unused computer terminal. The Guardian had already decided on what he dubbed the Argus Room. He thought the room's purpose of seeking extraterrestrial signals might mean that nobody paid strict attention to the room's network traffic, since nobody really expected an answer from space.

The Guardian walked past the doors behind which he'd seen Operation Atlantis, and crept around the corner. He met up with the eccentric tourists he'd snuck in with.

The stealth mode worked. Nobody paid any attention to him. Or maybe it didn't work, and they just thought he was dressed normally.

He couldn't remember which way to go next. Kevin laughed at himself. He could hear Will's voice from last years ill fated camping trip.

"You should always bring a map in the woods so you don't get lost and eaten by bears," it said.

Kevin had laughed at the time. Will was positive organization could save your life. Yet here he was. It was a dragon about to eat him but a map was what he needed.

The Guardian gasped as a map appeared suddenly on his visor. In fact, it was a complete set of blueprints. The Guardian wondered where the observatory was and a red line appeared like it was highlighting a route. With no better option, The Guardian decided to follow it. He found himself around the corner from the Operation Atlantis room.

As he looked around, his map rotated and showed blueprints for the area he was looking at. When he looked at the Operation Atlantis room, he noticed what appeared to be a secret passage marked on the map.

It was behind the tank filled with tropical fish that he had admired on the field trip only a few days ago. He made a mental note to investigate later.

He found the doors marked with the Mobius strip and star field. He pushed them open. Inside, was a small tour group being guided by Dr. Sharpe. Once again, nobody noticed The Guardian.

No one stopped him when he walked up to a terminal and, using the touch screen, started entering commands. It was the same terminal he had been examining when the power went out. It had a schematic of Argus.

The Guardian touched the terminal and carefully pictured the Argus terminal operating as a touch screen with a keyboard. He imagined it would gain him easy access to the Eureka Industries mainframe. A keyboard appeared along with a message welcoming him to the Eureka Industries computer network.

The armour was doing most of the work. The Guardian's fingers were almost moving on their own. Eventually the system challenged him, demanding the password.

The Guardian felt his heart racing. Why hadn't he thought of this? After everything he'd done he was going to be defeated by a simple precaution like a password.

He didn't know anyone's password and even with the suite's help, randomly trying to guess would likely set off alarms and catch him hacking the system.

The Guardian looked around desperately for inspiration, hoping to see something that would help him guess a correct password. He spotted Dr. Sharpe lecturing someone for touching a display. He grinned, realizing employees must have passwords. He concentrated on knowing the password for Brent Sharpe. Suddenly it appeared on his visor and his fingers typed it into his touch screen.

In minutes, he had access to top secret files. The Argus file showed that the new generation telescope was a revolutionary combination of space and radio telescope designed for more accurate scans of something called the point of signal and device origin.

The Guardian stared at this phrase. He wondered if it referred to his suit. Did this mean Eureka Industries didn't design it? Where did it come from?

He thought back to his conversation with Mr. Hill.

"The Braxton UFO urban legend is mostly true. Many people involved with that suit have died, including the original owner."

Kevin wondered if he was wearing an alien space suit.

He continued sorting through the Argus Files until he came across the plans for the telescope. The telescope required a huge amount of room for its construction, and for receiving the radio signals and other data it would send to earth. The file also noted that the observatory where data would be received would make an ideal location for elements of Project Taylor. The Guardian came across a file containing the list of properties under the heading of Obstacles for Removal.

The Guardian was appalled. This list contained buildings and properties to be purchased or destroyed in order to facilitate Project

Argus. The file didn't say who ordered this policy. The Guardian knew whoever it was could never be allowed to access the power he now possessed. This list contained houses, schools, rival businesses, businesses belonging to Eureka Industries, a retirement home and the new mall.

The Guardian downloaded these files into his suit. How he did this he wasn't exactly sure. All he knew was one minute he was reading the files on the monitor and then they were on his visor. He also downloaded them on to a disk he'd brought with him.

He quickly left the room. He now had provable evidence of the crimes going on.

The Guardian knew it was time to leave. As he reached the bathroom where he had applied his medicine and which provided easy access to the roof through a vent, he stopped in his tracks. He could hear voices from inside.

"Why are we meeting here Sheila?" The Dragon asked in a bored tone.

"Whoever stole my property was here. They destroyed this door. They've also been parading about playing hero. If you hadn't cleaned up Nigel, and I hadn't seen Michael outside when we sprung the trap, I'd think it was them.

I still think you should have torched the school. I could've seen more of this superhero's abilities. Do you have any idea who it is," said the voice The Guardian recognized as Helen Montgomery. She was talking as if she was ordering lunch.

"I have some leads but I can't share them with you. Like I'm always saying, you need deniability. This protects both of our businesses. Clients who don't trust me always get burned," The Dragon said softly.

There was a brief silence. When Helen Montgomery answered, her voice sent a shiver down The Guardian's spine.

"People who threaten me disappear. Project Taylor must proceed. I've let nothing stand in my way! Do whatever is necessary. If he doesn't hand it over, initiate the price," Helen said softly.

"I know your stakes. I will get your property. I have a plan. Do not however, think I'll disappear so easily. I know how to conduct business," The Dragon said.

There was a very uncomfortable silence. The Guardian was about to take the chance to leave. Hopefully, he'd be in time to avoid the violence that seemed likely to erupt in the bathroom. Then he heard a cell phone ring.

"Yes, what is it. I'm in a meeting. I see. Just like before. Prior to the blackout. Thank you. No. I will take care of the problem," Helen said sounding suddenly very happy as she hung up the phone.

"The cameras are on the fritz. Nothing but static on every screen. It started an hour ago. He's here. Find him."

CHAPTER FIFTEEN:
THE SECRET LAB

The Guardian thought fast. His enemies were about to walk right into him. They would probably hit him with the door when they left the bathroom. He spotted a mop and bucket leaning against the wall. He concentrated with all his might on the janitor uniform that he had seen The Dragon wearing when he had asked for directions to this very bathroom.

The Guardian heard the telltale whirring and clicking that meant the suit was responsive. He held his breath praying the sound couldn't be heard in the bathroom.

There was no pause in the instructions being given by Helen. The Guardian breathed a sigh of relief when he looked down and saw blue coveralls.

He ran, grabbed the mop and tried to lean casually against the wall. Or maybe he was using the wall and mop for support in case his knees gave way. Helen and The Dragon came out of the bathroom. They were having a continuing debate about how to proceed.

The Guardian held his breath, praying again that they wouldn't notice him. He hoped he hadn't flinched when Helen glanced in his direction. Unfortunately, something about him caught her attention. She stopped walking, turned to The Guardian and looked him up and down. She frowned slightly and raised her eyebrows.

"Have we met somewhere before? You look vaguely familiar," she said stepping closer.

"I don't think so ma'am. I just started here today. I've only been in town a couple of weeks," The Guardian said with a South African accent, inwardly thanking his drama teacher.

"My mistake. Carry on, but leave this bathroom for awhile. Some chemicals need to dissipate before it's safe to go in," Helen said, gesturing for The Dragon to follow her.

The Guardian reluctantly headed in the direction of the cafeteria carrying his new mop and bucket. He knew he was walking away from his best escape. He didn't want to risk the bathroom being watched. His second-best chance of getting out of here was probably just to walk out the front door using his new disguise or possibly blending in with another tour group.

The Guardian decided to take a page out of Dr. Hawthorne's book and get his evidence to someone else so it wasn't easily traceable to him. He decided to make life easier and present it to the person in the guise of The Guardian with clear instructions as to what to do with it.

The Guardian headed in the direction of the lobby. He intended to put his plan into action immediately. He thought of his costume and felt the armour activate. He activated the stealth mode. On his way past the Operation Atlantis room, the map appeared on his visor again.

Once again, The Guardian saw the clearly marked secret passage. Despite everything that had happened, his father's lessons and his desire for safe exit, the curiosity of a fifteen-year-old took over as he headed for the Operation Atlantis doors and pushed them open.

There was nobody inside. The only sounds were the steady buzz and bubbling of the fish tanks. Even being alone and for all practical purposes invisible, The Guardian felt the need to tiptoe to the fish tank that he had wanted to show to Will. He couldn't shake the feeling of being watched.

As he got closer, the secret passage on the map lined up perfectly with the tank. There was definitely something behind it. The Guardian was positive it was a door. How did he open it?

After examining the carved wooden paneling on the tank, he spotted something among the elaborately carved fish, weeds and bubbles. The Guardian originally thought it was a seashell between the two largest plants. He suddenly realized it was really the Eureka Industries logo turned sideways.

His curiosity intensified and The Guardian reached out to touch the Mobius strip. Before he could he became aware of someone behind him.

"Cool! You do exist!"

The Guardian spun around, expecting to see The Dragon. Instead he saw the guy with the tin foil hat that he had snuck in with.

"You're here to investigate the genetically engineered man-eating hamsters! Wait till I tell my buds!"

The Guardian realized his excitement had disabled the suit's stealth mode. He just shook his head. He wondered how many people like Alex lived in Braxton. He knew this was his opportunity. He reached into the pocket that suddenly appeared in the suit and held out the disk he'd downloaded his evidence onto.

"That's right you can help me by giving this disk to the cop with a huge beard who is named Cunningham.

Don't say it came from me and don't tell your buds about this. Keep it a secret between superhero and sidekick," The Guardian whispered.

"Awesome! You got it dude!" the would-be surfer dude said, pocketing the disk and sprinting from the room.

Against his better judgment, the moment he was alone, The Guardian reached out to the Mobius strip and pushed. Sure enough, the fish tank's glass front parted like elevator doors. The Guardian found himself standing at the entrance to a long dark corridor.

He took a step forward. The doors hissed closed. For a few seconds his footsteps echoed in the silence, only lightened by the gentle hum of the fish tank's air filters. After a little manoeuvring to avoid several booby traps and disabling a giant laser which fired out of one wall, The Guardian was almost blinded despite his visor's filtering abilities, when lights suddenly blazed from the ceiling.

The Guardian realized he was in a laboratory. He could see diagrams and schematics on the walls. Some of the pictures showed what looked like little robots. Or maybe they were molecules or cells. It was hard to tell. Test tubes, beakers and other lab equipment covered every surface.

A large tank or incubator stood in one corner. As The Guardian got closer he saw a collection of scalpels and other dissection equipment on the table. Next to these was a tape recorder. Above the table was a series of drawings and photographs that seemed to belong in a biology or anatomy textbook. The only problem was they contained body parts Kevin had never seen before.

The further The Guardian went into the lab, the more nervous and claustrophobic he became. The tape recorder, the musty smell and the silence gave him a sense that nobody had been here in a long time. The glass walls of the lab were made out of the sides of the fish tanks. Fish swam past him as he walked, giving him the feeling that he was on haunted shipwreck.

He tiptoed to the tape recorder. Knowing the sound would echo horribly, he held his breath as he pushed the play button. He half expected ghostly sailors to descend upon him. Instead the voice of the man Will bumped into issued from the speaker.

"This is Dr. Nigel Hawthorne recording observations of the nanotechnology device. I didn't believe Helen at first. The device could be extraterrestrial in origin. It contains elements which are not found on the periodic table or even in theoretical circles. My predecessor's notes on the device may confirm this. His other outlandish claims however, make this questionable," Dr. Hawthorne said sighing.

The Guardian wondered what these outlandish claims were. At this point he was willing to accept anything. He listened eagerly as Dr. Hawthorne's notes continued.

"Using the device on me indicates a number of enhancing abilities on the human body. These include enhancing physical strength, speed and endurance. The same holds true for the senses of hearing, sight and occasionally smell. Touch is unaffected. This is probably part of the device's protective function which also allows repair and healing of illness and injury.

Early tests indicate possibility of anti-gravity capability. This has not yet been confirmed through self-testing. It could be more exciting than other tests. I've always wanted to fly," Dr. Hawthorne said brightly.

The Guardian grumbled to himself about all the climbing he'd been doing. Flying would be a lot easier and more fun if he could bring himself to do it. He turned his attention back to the tape as Dr. Hawthorne's voice became troubled.

"If Helen's plans are what they appear to be and if my suspicions about the technology's capabilities are accurate, I fear for the consequences of my research particularly research in the area of replication."

On this ominous note the tape ended. The Guardian decided he'd pushed his luck far enough today. It was time to get out of here before somebody caught him. A familiar voice spoke behind him.

"I knew this room would catch your attention. I've been waiting for you."

The Guardian turned around slowly. A shiver went down his spine. He dreaded what he was going to see. Sure enough, The Dragon was blocking the entrance to the lab.

The Dragon smiled. He was wearing his flight goggles and jet pack again. This time the wings of the jet pack were extended, greatly increasing his resemblance to his namesake. He walked carefully down the passage, smiling more broadly the closer he got and making flames dance along his gloved fingers.

"Well, what have you decided? Shall I use fire to create or destroy today?" The Dragon asked softly.

The Guardian didn't answer. At first, he was terrified. He couldn't give his armour up. He was positive The Dragon would do terrible things whether he wanted it for himself or Helen Montgomery. He needed a way out fast. In answer to this desperate thought the blueprints appeared again, this time a complete blueprint of the skyscraper. He needed to keep his opponent talking, until he found an escape route.

"I'll never give it to you. Even your tiny lizard brain should be able to figure that out," The Guardian said, closely examining the blueprint.

The Dragon's face turned purple and he clenched his teeth. The flames along his fingers flared and he took several deep breaths before responding.

"Enough! This was supposed to be a simple business arrangement. You've interfered at every step. Instead of simply completing my art in the shadows and collecting my money quietly, I've been chasing after a freak who thinks he's a superhero! I was supposed to give you another chance! Give me the costume now!" The Dragon snarled.

The Guardian grinned behind his visor. He'd found his escape. He just needed to get his foe away from the exit. Thanks to his ranting, it was clear The Dragon was sensitive about professionalism.

"Aren't you curious about why I'm here? I have evidence that will put you and the dummy who hired an incompetent twit in prison," The Guardian said, laughing as loudly and obnoxiously as he could.

"Well, I'm willing to forgive your rudeness. It seems you're to have one more opportunity to do business. Give me your outfit and the evidence. I'll let you go if you do the smart thing," The Dragon said adopting a businesslike tone.

"Sorry it's already on the way to the cops! I guess you don't know when to close the deal! It's easy getting in your way. You feel the need to leave me finger paintings everywhere! Who told you that you were an artist? The kindergarten teacher before you flunked?" The Guardian asked in an annoyingly singsong voice.

The Dragon snapped. He charged at The Guardian, his gloves aflame, roaring in a very dragon-like way. The Guardian was ready. He sprang away from the table, grabbed The Dragon by the arm, using their combined momentum to send the mercenary over the table and crashing into the display of anatomy diagrams.

Without pausing to see his handiwork, The Guardian dashed down the corridor, activating the stealth and interference modes as he went. He slammed his palm on the Mobius symbol and sprinted past two unseeing security guards.

He turned the corner and saw the unused hallway he'd noticed on the blueprints. They'd showed him an old elevator at the end of the hall. The Guardian skidded to a stop, disappointed. Nothing was there but a cement wall. He decided to test the extent of his superpowers and punched the wall as hard as he could.

The wall crumpled like tissue paper. The Guardian beamed. He was now standing in front of an elevator door. He pushed the down button and ran inside. The smashing wall must have gotten somebody's attention. As he went to push the loading zone button, he realized he needed a security card to use the elevator. He was trapped.

The Guardian had an idea. If his armour did operate on nanotechnology maybe he wasn't stuck. He placed his hand on the elevator panel, concentrating on sending some nanites to override the security program. The card reader turned green.

Kevin pushed the button for the loading dock and minutes later he was on the street waiting for a bus. He looked at his watch. Kevin couldn't believe he'd only been at Eureka Industries for two hours. Merlin wouldn't even miss his lunchtime walk.

CHAPTER SIXTEEN:
THE GRAND OPENING

Kevin woke up in a good mood. He had broken into The Dragon's den and escaped. He'd gathered evidence connecting the arsons to someone at the company. His evidence was safely on the way to the police and the armour was safe. Maybe now everything would go back to normal.

Kevin was conflicted about what to do next. Part of him felt Braxton still needed The Guardian. His suit and persona had helped people and made Braxton a better and safer town. The other part of his mind argued The Guardian had increased the danger.

He knew that the abilities provided by the suit had saved Carol and Alex and had stopped The Dragon when the police around the world couldn't. His dad always said when a case was closed; move on.

Kevin decided to put all these concerns aside for now. Today he was supposed to meet Will for the official grand opening of the Braxton Shopping Center. They were going to meet in three hours. After playing with Merlin, Kevin decided to watch TV.

There was almost nothing on, except for the specialty channels. All the other channels were featuring the same special report. Each channel had a background picture of the mall, with a crowd of bickering people who were waiting to shop. The only thing that convinced Kevin the remote was working was seeing the different reporters. The reporters even said pretty much the same thing. He decided to watch the report by Ben Simmons.

"We are coming live from the Canadian city of Braxton. This community's former claim to fame was being home to the fast food restaurant Cowboy Tom's Family Feed Bag. However, restaurant founder Thomas Henry Braxton would eventually relocate headquarters to seek the destiny indicated by his hotline psychic," the reporter said smiling.

Kevin stared at the TV in amazement. No wonder the information regarding the official biography of the school's namesake in the student handbook was vague.

"The city hoped to recoup business losses and overcome its reputation for strange events by building a shopping center which will be the largest in the world. In addition to stores and restaurants, the mall will feature I Max theatres. There will also be a theme park." Ben Simmons said in a bored voice.

Ben Simmons unlike the other excitable reporters Kevin had watched had no interest in this story. He talked about the mall in the same tone somebody might use to describe paint drying.

"Although the mall opened months ago, preparations for this grand opening are intended to introduce the shopping center to the world. As part of this effort at cleaning up of the city's image, dignitaries from the city, province and all over the world have been invited. It is hoped the numbers in attendance will reach several thousand. The dignitaries have been assured that neither the mysterious vigilante nor arsons will interfere with the ceremony," Ben Simmons said, his voice brightening.

Kevin heaved a sigh of relief. He'd stopped The Dragon just in time. This grand opening would have been the perfect time to cause the chaos he'd threatened. If Kevin had been just a day later, hundreds of people could have been dead.

Kevin went up to his bedroom. There was something that had been intriguing and terrifying him since he got back from Eureka Industries. Could he really fly?

Dr. Hawthorne had speculated that Kevin possessed a space suit. Kevin supposed anti-gravity properties made sense. Testing this involved obvious risk and excitement. This was extra complicated because Kevin was afraid of heights.

He decided to start small. He stood on his bed and activated the armour, his eyes tightly shut as he muttered to himself.

"I will just levitate off the bed. I will not drop like a stone. I'm not going to die. The bed is soft. I want to do this. It is safe," Kevin said fully aware of his racing heart, sweaty palms and treacherously trembling voice.

Kevin held his breath. Nothing happened. As he sighed in relief, he suddenly no longer felt the reassuring firmness of his mattress under his feet. He opened his eyes and saw his bed below him. He counted to ten before looking around to confirm his impossible position. He was startled to see the ceiling fan centimetres from his head.

"I have to get down!" he blurted out, concentrating with all his might on landing on the bed.

Instead of floating gently down Kevin shot sideways like he'd been blasted out of a cannon. He tried to veer off and avoid the bookshelf next to his bed. Instead, he smashed into it. Kevin was covered in an avalanche of textbooks, his comic book collection and twelve box sets of *Tales of Chivalry*.

"Kevin Oliver Rigby if you're going to jump on the bed and demolish the house go play outside!" his mother called from downstairs in a half exasperated half amused voice.

Kevin groaned as pushed himself up from the ground for the twelfth time. He glared up at the evil tree house. For at least an hour he'd jumped off his old tree house to test his anti-gravity abilities. They had failed miserably. He could float in the sky for a few seconds but then he'd smash into this stupid spot.

Merlin padded over, sniffing Kevin meticulously from armoured head to foot. His tail drooped. He whined, sat down and cocked his head, looking quizzically at Kevin.

"You're right Merlin I'm crazy," Kevin said, petting the dog as he rummaged through his backpack for his ringing cell phone.

"Hey Will, what's up?" Kevin asked automatically.

"Hi Kev. I just wanted to tell you to bring your school ID when you come to the mall," Will said cheerfully.

"Why? It's hideous and looks nothing like me." Kevin answered.

"Student ID of any kind will get us discounts!" Will said, his tone making Kevin positive he was bouncing up and down.

"Okay I'll see you in a minute. I just have to put Merlin in the house."

"Sure. By the way have you heard from Alex today? I was going to invite him but I can't find him. His parents aren't home as usual. He's not answering the phone or his e-mail. He is obsessive about that," Will said sounding puzzled and worried.

"Maybe we'll run into him when we get there and you guys can have another debate," Kevin said laughing.

An hour later, Kevin and Will arrived at the Braxton Shopping Center. Kevin couldn't believe his eyes. The place was huge. He hadn't really noticed this when he'd been there buying Will's birthday present. He noticed the mall's size now because it was so crowded. Customers bustled off in every direction, often pushing past reporters and TV crews. There were animal acts and theme park rides in addition to the stores and kiosks.

For a while Kevin and Will simply wandered around in a daze. The maps they bought were no help. Each map was so big that when they opened it, it wasn't possible see where you were going and read them at the same time.

They spotted many other Braxton High students. Kevin noticed everybody was carrying their school ID. They kept an eye out for Alex but didn't see him anywhere. They did see Travis with a couple of his goons. To Kevin's amazement they ran into Mindy working at Comic Universe.

"Excuse me, where can I find the Manga section?" Kevin asked doubtfully.

Mindy looked at Kevin as if he'd just burst out in Martian or vomited on the floor.

"Do I look like I know what Mango is?"

"Manga. It's Japanese comics like Astro Boy.

"I don't care," Mindy said with a huge fake yawn.

"How did you even get this job?" Kevin demanded.

"The Manager thinks I'll attract customers. Particularly awkward geeks like you," Mindy replied opening a fashion magazine and disappearing behind it.

Kevin was going to respond in outrage but looking around the store he grudgingly thought the manager was right. The crowd around him was mostly made of teenage boys. Will was the only one currently not shooting glances at Mindy and him. He noticed some were glaring jealously at him!

Shuddering, Kevin joined Will in front of a vintage comic display. Kevin wondered if he was blushing or green. Either way he was glad he didn't have a mirror. Will's hysterical laughter was bad enough.

"Wow! A three hundred dollar first edition," Kevin said hoping for a distraction.

Next, they went to the photography store. Kevin wasn't very impressed. He'd worked on two yearbooks. These cameras were all flash and no substance. Will however was in heaven. He quickly selected a camera that looked like it was from outer space. He skipped over to the counter flashing his student ID.

"Who are you kidding kid? Do you have thousands of dollars? This discount can't help you," the cashier said sneering at the ID.

Will dragged Kevin from the store so fast Kevin thought he'd left his feet behind. Kevin gently steered Will in the direction of the food court. Will was so dejected he didn't even react when Kevin theatrically ripped up the Fabulous Photos brochure before tossing the pieces in the garbage can which startled them when it spoke in a Scottish accent.

"Thank you. You're a bonnie person for keeping the center clean."

Kevin and Will joined the line in front of a Chinese restaurant. Will was revived somewhat by the smell of his favourite food. He looked around, cheerfully humming to himself. Suddenly, he nudged Kevin in the ribs.

"Look out, here comes Travis," he whispered urgently.

"It's okay I've tamed my bully," Kevin said smiling and waving Travis over.

"Hi what are you guys doing?" Travis asked brightly.

Will gazed blankly between Kevin and Travis, clearly wondering about this new level of interaction. He looked around cautiously. Kevin knew he was looking for Travis' friends. When he was satisfied it was safe, he answered Travis.

"Having lunch and I for one have no intention of paying full price."

Will pulled his wallet out with a flourish. His grin vanished as he thumbed through it.

"I lost my ID! I must have dropped it! You have to pay for a new one. I'm dead!" Will said frantically searching his pockets.

Kevin could see one of Will's patented unorganized panic attacks coming on. He had to act fast. Luckily, he had a good a hunch about the location of the student identification.

"I'll get it. Just relax and order me the chicken balls and rice combo," he said, tapping Will's shoulder.

The mall was so crowded Kevin took fifteen minutes to find his way back to Fabulous Photos. When he asked about student identifications, the cashier was grumpy. He brought back a gigantic box and dumped a mountain of ID's and driver's licenses on the counter.

"What a stupid promotion! You'd think people would remember these things! Find it and get lost!" he snapped grinding his teeth.

Kevin found Will's ID and left the store, thinking that one store would soon be closing. He was halfway to the food court when panicked shouts suddenly erupted. Kevin froze even as his suit activated. He heard a calm voice over the intercom but it didn't give evacuation instructions.

"Attention all local vigilantes. Please bring the package I requested to the food court or we'll start the world's largest barbecue without you. Unfortunately, we only have three shrimp," The Dragon said blandly.

Forgetting to activate the stealth mode, The Guardian raced for the food court. The reporters saw him and raced to follow him with their cameraman panting behind them.

The Guardian dashed into the food court. His worst fears were confirmed when he saw no sign of Travis or Will; only a spilled tray of Chinese food and an overturned table.

The Dragon stood calmly on a second table as if it were a stage. He spread out his arms and smiled as the TV crews arrived.

"Welcome ladies and gentlemen. You are about to see a real-life confrontation between superhero and super villain. The only question is which is which…"

His speech was cut short when The Guardian launched himself across the table and threw him to the floor. The Dragon smiled, as he pushed The Guardian off him.

"Where are they?" The Guardian bellowed.

"Temper mate. I told you this was just business. You've gone and lost control. You've revealed that you're not one of the hostages I snatched. Don't worry; I won't have you reveal your secrets here. I'll give you a last chance," The Dragon said calmly while kicking The Guardian in the ribs.

The Guardian struggled to his feet. He was amazed by how calm he was. Maybe the suit relaxed his mind like it healed him. Or maybe he just realized his enemy was trying to provoke him like he'd done to him at Eureka Industries.

"If it's just business why not tell me where they are?" The Guardian urged.

Instead of answering, The Dragon walked over to the spilled food tray and dropped something on it. His jet pack came to life with a humming sound, wings extended. He rocketed upward smashing through the food court's glass ceiling.

"See you around mate. Remember you could have stopped this." The Dragon pointed a remote towards the spilled Chinese food.

"Bomb!" somebody yelled.

The Guardian had to fight his way through the terrified reporters to reach the overturned table. He seized the bowling ball sized object on the tray and followed The Dragon's escape route through the skylight by climbing on the table and jumping through the broken glass roof.

Somewhere in the back of his mind he registered that the blood red timer had reached three seconds as he plummeted into a dumpster.

No explosion came. Instead the bomb hissed open with a puff of smoke. Kevin blinked. It was hollow. He could see two things inside it. One was a *Mr. Soapy's Cleaning Service* business card with an address.

Kevin's stomach dropped when he turned over the second object. He recognized it as student identification for Braxton High. When he saw the name on it he wondered if HE was the super villain. It read: **Alexander Jason Moor.**

. . . .

An hour later, Kevin sat dejectedly on his bed. His mom had sent him to sleep. She'd told him there was nothing he could do for Will and the others. The Dragon's business card had politely reminded Kevin the hostages would die if he missed the meeting.

Kevin glumly flipped through the photos from Will's birthday. He came across the picture taken just after he had pulled Alex from the swimming pool. He'd been so proud he'd smiled even as he stood shivering between Will and Alex.

Now, Kevin knew he'd done nothing. Sure, he jumped in the pool but the suit was responsible for his rescue. The Dragon started more fires because of him. Kevin wasn't a superhero. The news reports were right. He was a menace.

The Dragon was right too. He could stop this. Why shouldn't he give up the suit?

The photo in Kevin's hand faded. He was hurtling through space. He didn't know who he was.

CHAPTER SEVENTEEN: JULY FIFTEENTH

The Searcher knew he was badly wounded and wouldn't last much longer. The Cocoon had already enveloped him but the nanites were having trouble making repairs. Not only had he been injured in the meteor shower, The Cocoon indicated that it had been damaged. The Searcher's injuries and the repairs of The Cocoon were proving difficult for the nanites. The readout indicated that a planetary environment was necessary for the proper healing of both.

The Searcher initiated a scan, activated the protocol override, went into Hibernation Mode and switched on automatic record and flight. Earth appeared on the readout and Kevin found he could still see the readout even though he no longer identified with The Searcher's thoughts.

The next image Kevin saw was a flash of blue light and he heard a brief rushing sound as if he were speeding down a tunnel. He saw a star-filled night sky that was briefly illuminated by a bright flash of the same light as he'd seen in the tunnel. The recording showed stars spiraling past, then the floor of the forest below and dirt and rocks spraying into the sky. Kevin guessed that The Cocoon had entered the atmosphere and impacted like a meteorite.

. . . .

For a while Kevin could see only trees and grass. It felt as if he was really standing in the middle of the clearing The Cocoon had made in the forest. Soon police cars arrived and five cops with flashlights got out and started looking around. Shortly afterwards, several black vans with Mobius symbols on the side showed up. All kinds of people in hazmat suits carrying a lot of equipment got out of the vans and started rushing around.

"What's going on here? You can't just run around destroying evidence in an investigation," a young officer said heatedly, sprinting up to the people in environmental suits.

Nobody paid any attention to the young cop. They just kept doing what they were doing. The cop was obviously mad. He kept repeating his demands for an explanation, called the other police over to help him and even started pointing at his badge.

Two people got out of one of the black vans and approached the young officer. They were wearing black suits and each had Eureka Industries name tags.

"Good evening Officer. I'm Dr. Michael Hill and I'm in charge of this research facility. We're sorry if our tests caused uproar. Everything's under control here and poses no danger. Your people may leave now," one of the men said.

The young officer stood his ground and carefully looked the men up and down. When he responded, it was with a nod and a polite but firm tone. It was the kind of voice that usually left no one doubt about who was in charge. He pointed in the direction of the trees where the object had impacted.

"We're not going anywhere! Your research hasn't just caused an uproar. There is a huge crater and one patrolman told me there was something moving inside," he said, glaring at them for good measure.

"Really Gentleman there is no reason to become territorial."

The three men looked around, wearing expressions that suggested they had forgotten anyone else was there. The newcomer was a young woman in her late teens or early twenties. Her sparkling dress and diamond necklace looked like they belonged at the prom or a formal dinner. She smiled at the young officer.

"My name is Helen Montgomery, Officer. I assure you the police will have our full cooperation. In the meantime, I must ask you to leave. The research here is of a sensitive nature. Because of your lack of expertise, your presence is more dangerous than the research itself." Helen Montgomery made this speech in a warm friendly tone, with a big smile that didn't reach her eyes.

The young officer protested some more but a senior officer with a buzz cut and goatee arrived and took charge of the scene. This officer immediately gave in to Helen's requests and led the young officer over to the line of patrol cars.

"Why are we are giving in to her, Officer Cunningham? Something is definitely going on. All those reports definitely indicated witnesses seeing something in the sky, and before they showed up I know I saw a crater," the young officer said glaring in Helen's direction.

"Calm down Matt. It is private property and she's right. If we go poking around, it'll do more than harm good," Officer Cunningham said clapping the other cop on the shoulder.

"Something is going on James. I'm going to figure out what they're up to," the young officer said squaring his shoulders.

"Just be careful. Helen Montgomery has a lot of influence. You don't want to get in her crosshairs," Officer Cunningham said as they got into a police car.

. . . .

Helen watched the police cars until they were out of sight. Then, beaming and with a gleam in her eye, she turned to her team.

"Now that those fools are gone, I want to see what your satellites picked up. It had better be worth interrupting my date with Ned. Lead on," she said gesturing at Dr. Hill to walk in front of her.

Dr. Hill led her through the forest to a large crater which had been roped off by the technicians that had arrived in the vans. She pushed past a pair of these technicians to peer down into the crater. Kevin couldn't see whatever she did because from the perspective of his suit she was standing right above him. Whatever she saw must've been impressive because she smiled.

"There's some kind of creature. It's been encapsulated in some sort of armour. It doesn't look very healthy. I think I can see what might be blood," Helen said in a casually interested sort of way.

"We should get it out of there and see if we can help," Dr. Hill said as he joined Helen at the crater rim.

"Yes. Get it away from here before more people come snooping. As for helping it, we'll see about that later," Helen said smiling and patting Dr. Hill on the back.

As he turned away to direct the technicians, Helen Montgomery's smile widened. As she headed back to her limousine, she started humming. Eventually Dr. Hill caught up with her.

"What do we do now ma'am?" he asked.

"First we get rid of all these reporters. We acknowledge nothing and let the UFO nuts babble. No one takes them seriously anyway. We keep a low profile and infiltrate the police investigation.

My family has been watching the skies ever since a certain incident in New Mexico. If I'm right, when the world wakes up tomorrow nothing will be the same," she said in the same chilling voice she had used when she'd been instructing The Dragon.

• • • • • • • • • •

The scene before Kevin eyes shifted, and he saw Helen Montgomery and Dr. Hill standing in the secret laboratory. Kevin knew this because it looked like fish swam all around them as if they and their equipment were under water.

"Are you sure it's safe keeping the patient here?" Dr. Hill whispered as if he worried about being overhead.

Helen Montgomery laughed loudly, patting Dr. Hill on the shoulder. She gave him a reassuring smile. When she addressed him, her tone suggested he was an over-excited child.

"Nobody who could cause trouble knows about the specimen. Besides, even if they did, they couldn't find us here," she said, calmly gesturing at the bizarre setting.

Dr. Hill nodded but he didn't look convinced.

"What is the status of the specimen?" Helen Montgomery demanded.

Dr. Hill frowned slightly, either considering his answer or because he didn't like the word specimen. Helen repeated herself sharply and stared down Dr. Hill.

"The patient appears to be injured and in a low functioning state. I believe this is to allow the nanotechnology to repair the damage. The device appears to be attached to the patient and able to effect the entire body through an interface with the brain," Dr. Hill said excitedly.

"Is there any way to determine the full abilities of the interface?" Helen asked, moving to stand over The Searcher. Kevin could tell she was examining The Searcher like he would examine a microscope slide in class.

"The only way to know for sure is to test the device on an organism we understand better. The device is directly interfaced to the brain. It is acting as a space suit or ship. I think removing it would kill the patient."

Helen Montgomery nodded. She picked up a lab instrument and stabbed The Searcher; killing it. Dr. Hill stood with his mouth hanging open. Helen on the other hand calmly sat down in a chair folding her hands in her lap.

"Don't look so shocked Michael. It was probably an alien equivalent to the chimps or dogs we use in space. Life forms of lesser value are always early test subjects. If it was an explorer he chose a dangerous profession. Our own Age of Exploration brought disease, death and war. These are the price of the knowledge. If your anatomy theories are right, your exploration is about to begin." Helen Montgomery smiled again as she took out a clipboard and waited.

• • • • • • • • • •

The scene before Kevin eyes shifted. He saw Helen Montgomery standing with a younger Nigel Hawthorne. They were standing in the Operation Atlantis room.

"Thank you for coming Nigel. I've spent a long time trying to find you. I promise that this will prove worth my efforts and your time," Helen said beaming at Nigel.

"I must say Helen, I'm not sure if I believe you. Your guarantees seem too good to be true but I couldn't resist," Nigel said bouncing on his toes.

Helen Montgomery didn't answer. She just walked over to one of the fish tanks and pressed her thumb into the carved wood surrounding it. The tanks split open, revealing the door into the secret laboratory.

Helen gestured the stunned looking Nigel to go ahead of her. When she walked into the laboratory, she took off a necklace she'd been wearing and set it on the table. The necklace twisted for an instant until the compact version of Kevin's suit appeared. Helen turned to grin at the stunned Nigel.

"I found it by following your reported signals. I assume you've heard of the Braxton UFO story. It's true. There was a light in the sky and when my people arrived we saw a crater and found this," she said handing the device to Nigel.

"The signals are extraterrestrial in origin! I knew it!" Nigel Hawthorne said peering hungrily at the object in his hand.

"Yes they certainly are. This device operates using nanotechnology. So far, we know that it heals injuries and some forms of illness, increases the user's strength, changes shape, responds to thought and could even function as a spaceship. If you help me unlock its roots,

I guarantee you Cambridge will be sorry they fired you," Helen said putting her arm around Dr. Hawthorne shoulder. He smiled at her with tears in his eyes.

• • • • • • • • • •

The scene shifted again. Dr. Hawthorne was standing in a different laboratory looking through a microscope and wearing the suit around his neck. He looked up and a few minutes later footsteps could be heard. Helen Montgomery walked through the door.

"Any progress Nigel?" she asked.

"None. I managed to make the first copy using the information in the database but the nanites won't divide again. The override I managed to build in disappeared. I can't reactivate it. I think it's a safety measure. I'm guessing the designers didn't want this technology copied," Nigel said glaring at the microscope as though it was responsible for his lack of success.

"Whatever they wanted, I want those copies! The mass production of this technology will be the greatest achievement since the invention of the wheel. It will change the world," Helen said her eyes shining.

Nigel Hawthorne didn't look convinced. He was fidgeting and running his hand through his hair. Helen went over to him and placed both her hands on his shoulders and leaned in until they were nose to nose.

"Think Nigel. This is your redemption, your chance to prove all those people who laughed at you wrong. You used to teach at Oxford and Cambridge. When I found you, you were in academic exile wondering around The Sakha Republic and Siberia. Help me, and we change the world and you become the greatest thinker since Leonardo Da Vinci."

Nigel Hawthorne nodded. The manic gleam in Helen's eyes appeared in his.

• • • • • • • • • •

Ignoring the luxurious surroundings of Helen's office, Nigel Hawthorne paced before Helen's desk. She seemed amused as she sat watching him behind her enormous desk in the red leather chair.

"I've told you before Nigel, that the tour groups are going to continue. Operating in the dark invites rumour mongering and irritating snooping. We have to show a public face. Have you managed to copy the technology yet?" she asked sounding bored.

"No, the original still won't divide again and the first copy doesn't seem to have the ability to replicate its nanites. It's also unstable and unpredictable. I don't dare risk testing the device on humans. I also can't guarantee everyone's safety. I'm very worried about the consequences of an accident around these tour groups; especially with the children," he said continuing to pace, running his hand through his hair.

"There is no advancement without risk Nigel. Mass production of the device will change the world in ways not seen since Prometheus stole fire and gave it to mortals. We will be the new gods! I'm prepared to risk anything," Helen said coldly.

Nigel didn't answer. He understood the kind of change his former student planned all too well. The Cocoon had shown him. Helen had no idea it could access her database with ease. She thought it only gave her access to alien knowledge. He knew about the global recruitment trip she'd taken which included mercenaries as well as scientists. He could prove the identity of one mercenary. He doubted the janitor recognized him but he remembered Wes Howard. He turned to leave the office.

"Nigel I always clean up my messes. Ask the science teacher on your way back to work," she called out laughing as he shut the door.

Nigel shivered. He couldn't believe Helen was his former student. He knew she would act quickly. Luckily for him he had acted faster. The cameras were already disabled. He had access to the power systems, and was wearing the compacted device. The only problem was he didn't have time to get the copy but Helen knew it was unstable and would create a weapon she couldn't use, would turn against her or cause a public display she didn't want.

Nigel smiled to himself because thanks to the suit's database he'd made absolutely certain she couldn't replicate the first copy. Her mercenaries would not use alien technology to change the world.

Although the tour groups did prevent public speculation and urban legends, they also prevented her from acting too fast. He still had time to stop her. That was when he saw four boys heading for the public toilets.

CHAPTER EIGHTEEN:
THE PICTURE AND THE DAMSEL

TWO HOURS AGO...

The photographs fell to the floor. The sound of them bouncing off his stack of *Tales of Chivalry* books brought Kevin back to the present and the realization that he was not Nigel Hawthorne. Kevin's dilemma returned, along with this realization. What he had just seen and experienced, he didn't fully understand. He did know neither Helen Montgomery nor The Dragon could possess his armour or the power it granted people.

Kevin knew The Searcher had been worried about the possible consequences and dangers of making repairs and recovering on Earth. Kevin hadn't understood all of the alien's concerns but he knew Helen Montgomery had killed not only The Searcher but several others to take possession of the alien technology. Kevin thought that he alone understood the tempting possibilities that the armour offered.

The way Helen talked about the technology reminded Kevin of some of the more extreme religion and politics professors Aunt Leona worked with. The future consequences of any mass production of his armour made Kevin want to cry.

Kevin was distracted from his seemingly impossible puzzle when Merlin pushed his door open and jumped on the bed. Merlin wrapped himself around Kevin's legs, settling in for a nap.

"Am I the right person to keep it?" Kevin asked, scratching Merlin behind his ears.

Merlin just yawned and flipped over waving his paw. Kevin obligingly started rubbing Merlin's tummy. He leaned over the edge of the bed. Something on the floor had caught his attention.

It was the picture of Will and Alex standing on either side of him after he'd rescued Alex from the pool. As Kevin looked at the photo he realized he wasn't wearing anything around his neck; only the towel wrapped around his shoulders. Will's grumpy voice came back to Kevin, as if he was still sitting poolside watching Travis and his fellow party crashers.

"You'd better put that away before Travis or his goons steal it."

Feeling a thrill of excitement Kevin jumped up from bed and rummaged frantically through his dresser. He found the compacted suit still looking like a gold necklace with a pendent. He grinned as he put it around his neck. The suit wasn't responsible for his first rescue. He'd done that all by himself!

The Guardian was no longer idle and moping. He was a knight on his way to save three damsels. He was passing the playground when he heard the disturbingly familiar sound of Carol's voice calling for help.

The Guardian felt a horrified jolt in the pit of his stomach as he ran towards Carol's voice. She had heard The Dragon speak and he always cleaned up his messes. The Guardian ran as fast as he could until he found Carol standing under a tree. He looked around frantically even checking out the sky in case The Dragon had flown in. He didn't see anything except for Carol. She was sobbing but otherwise seemed fine.

The Guardian decided to take a direct approach. He deactivated the stealth mode. He approached the little girl cautiously, so he wouldn't startle her and spoke just loud enough for her to hear.

"What's wrong Carol?" he whispered in her ear.

Carol wiped her eyes and turned around.

"Mr. Snuggles is stuck up there. Please get him down Kevin," Carol said.

Kevin laughed. She had known it was him during the fire after all. He nodded, climbed the tree and retrieved the distressed kitten. He concentrated on gently floating down with the kitten nestled safely against his chest and amazingly felt his feet make gentle contact with the ground. He handed Mr. Snuggles to Carol.

"Thank you Kevin. Why are you wearing a Halloween costume?" Carol asked indicating the suit.

"It lets me help keep people safe. Like when I saved you from the closet. I have to keep it secret because if anyone knew I couldn't do that," Kevin answered realizing for the first time he'd decided to keep the suit after was this over.

"People at school tell me superheroes don't exist. I almost believed them," Carol said smiling.

The Guardian stood on the roof across from the address that The Dragon had given him. It was a large warehouse. Thanks to the enhanced sight and display provided by his visor The Guardian could see at least four guards. From Dr. Hawthorne's memories, he knew Helen had hired many more mercenaries. The display also showed what looked like heat signatures on the roof, at the windows and doors. This would be like running an obstacle course. The Guardian didn't bother with the stealth mode. It was time to save his friends and for The Dragon to learn what it was like to deal with a superhero.

• • • • • • • • • •

THE PRESENT SOMEWHERE NEAR THE WAREHOUSE...

Helen Montgomery leaned back in her plush leather chair and calmly sipped her tea. She watched the figure on her TV screen with admiration. The figure moved with absolute silence even as he ran across rooftops. The figure had climbed onto this roof after appearing in midair and landing on a building with a connecting roof.

A guard standing at the base of the parking structure was taken out without even noticing the figure above his head. The figure known as The Guardian was climbing buildings and running like a mountain goat.

"Impressive isn't it Peter. Continue monitoring the approximate speed and agility of the target please," Helen said to a short stocky scientist beside her.

She took another sip of tea. Soon, she would have not only the extraterrestrial device but the specimen that had unlocked the technology's secrets.

"Today's the day the world is changed forever. Nothing stands in my way," Helen said smiling.

CHAPTER NINETEEN:
THE KNIGHT AND THE DRAGON

NOW...

The Guardian edged carefully around the innocent looking air conditioner on the roof of the warehouse. According to the readout from the suit it was rigged with enough explosives to set half the block ablaze. Unfortunately, it was also in the middle of the only safe route to the hostages. The Guardian tiptoed toward the fire escape door. He knew it had to be a trap. Every other entrance had been secured either by a mercenary or a bomb meant to explode when either the window or door was opened. He placed his hand on the air conditioner and concentrated like he had in the elevator at Eureka Industries.

Expecting an explosion, The Guardian held his breath as he reached for the door. Nothing happened. His hand was on the handle when he heard voices and running footsteps on the other side.

Thinking quickly, The Guardian backed away from the door, activating the stealth mode as he went. He was just in time. Somebody shouted and the door opened. Someone sprinted out the door. In the light spilling outside, he recognized Travis.

"Get back here kid!" yelled an irritatingly familiar voice.

Mr. Knife charged out of the door brandishing his signature weapon.

The Guardian couldn't help sighing. *This was getting boring*. Still invisible, he stepped between Travis and Mr. Knife.

"You're not going anywhere. Nothing would please me more than to carve you up. Lucky for you there's still half an hour until the boss's deadline Get over here!" Mr. Knife ordered, waving Travis over with his weapon.

Travis took a terrified step towards Mr. Knife who leered at him and beckoned with his knife again.

"How many times do we have to do this?" The Guardian asked, disabling the stealth mode.

Mr. Knife's eyes flashed with rage and hate. The Guardian was amazed when Mr. Knife screamed in an almost primal way before hurling his knife at his chest.

The Guardian watched the knife coming directly for his heart. Knowing it was hopeless, he raised his hand. Amazingly he caught the knife in midair. Breathing a sigh of relief, he threw it over the side of the roof.

Both Travis and Mr. Knife stared at The Guardian in astonishment. Then Mr. Knife charged. The Guardian grabbed the mercenary and punched him. He dropped Mr. Knife as he slumped to the ground.

The Guardian bent down to check Mr. Knife's pockets and found three more weapons, some keys, a detonator and a rope inside his jacket. He smashed the detonator and broke two of the knives. He kept one for freeing Will and Alex. He hogtied the mercenary.

"Where did you come from?" Travis demanded.

"Never mind Travis! Just go get help! I assume that was your original idea," The Guardian said, nudging his former bully to get him started.

Travis turned around and began walking away. He'd only gone a few steps when he came back, looking sheepishly at his feet which reminded the would-be superhero of the fateful trip to the bathroom.

"Um how do I get down?" Travis asked his sneakers.

"Oh right, sorry you can't fly," The Guardian said feeling very glad his helmet hid his blushing.

Unfortunately, The Guardian could only think of one thing to do. He knew this suggestion wasn't going to be well received. Biding his time, he walked slowly over to Travis.

"I'm going to carry you," he said quickly, hoping to prevent his statement from sinking in too fast.

"No way dude!" Travis said looking mortified.

"Okay, I guess you could just wait for your friend to wake up or the guy in the flight goggles to show up again," The Guardian said brightly, nodding towards the hogtied Mr. Knife.

Travis glanced at Mr. Knife shuddered and nodded. Without further ado, The Guardian scooped Travis into his arms. He was sure his face bore the same look of shock Travis had, about how easy it was to pick him up.

"Welcome to Superhero Airline. All passengers please hold on tight and don't look down." The Guardian said, stepping nervously off the edge of the roof.

Travis screamed. He'd looked down. He was the same sinister shade of green he'd been two weeks ago. The Guardian once again thought of the unfortunate consequences of this complexion and Travis moaned ominously. The Guardian increased their descent as much as he dared. Travis was turning greener by the second. Thankfully, they reached the ground just in time. The Guardian put Travis down just before he vomited. He looked like he was about to collapse.

"No time for that. You have to get help now!" The Guardian said, steadying Travis.

"I'll be back as soon as I can!" Travis said and without looking back he ran down the street with the speed only an obsessive athlete could muster.

The Guardian launched himself upwards, knowing two hostages were still in danger. Time was running out. He had a feeling he was being watched. Looking around he couldn't see anyone. He knew things were going too easily when he landed on the warehouse roof without incident. Suddenly, he heard distinctive hum of a jet pack and a voice calling from somewhere above him.

"Well done mate. Why don't you come up here and get me!"

Across the street, The Dragon was floating in midair. He'd been hiding behind a factory smokestack. Circling the rooftop, he smiled down at The Guardian. The Guardian thought the super villain was showing off. He kept flying in circles and performing airborne acrobatics. The Guardian realized he was being deliberately mocked in order to draw him away from his friends.

Ignoring The Dragon's taunts, The Guardian carefully opened the door on the warehouse roof and went inside. The warehouse was pitch black. The Guardian proceeded cautiously down the stairs. He knew this was too easy. There had been no explosives or guards. If the last two weeks proved anything, it was that he wasn't this lucky.

Sure enough, when he reached the bottom of the stairs a baseball bat whizzed through the air where The Guardian's head had been seconds before. He was ready. He grabbed the bat just as the lights flared in an obvious attempt to blind him.

The Guardian managed to flip over Bat Boy and disarm him. A second bat connected with his head. He blinked. Everything was upside down. He realized as he saw somebody's feet that he was laying down. The second attack had come from above. With his wings retracting into his jetpack and holding a bat, The Dragon was standing over The Guardian.

"Stop! Don't hurt him!" somebody yelled.

Looking across the room, The Guardian saw Will and Alex. Each hostage was chained to a pillar and a bomb on opposite sides of the warehouse. For some reason, there was a big screen TV between them.

"On your feet hero! One last chance! Give me what I want now and you all leave in safety. Both children are chained to bombs! Choose quickly!" The Dragon said while helping The Guardian to his feet.

The Dragon pressed a button on his gauntlet. The Guardian held his breath as he braced himself to die with his friends.

Nothing happened. The Guardian looked around in relief until he saw the television screen. An unmistakable countdown of ten minutes appeared there. Underneath the quickly diminishing countdown appeared an animated dragon. The dragon roared and flames erupted behind Kevin with a tremendous bang as a huge piece of the roof fell, blocking the fire escape.

"Does that look like finger paintings to you mate?" The Dragon asked smiling coldly.

CHAPTER TWENTY:
THE HERO

The Guardian stood frozen and watched the countdown in horror. He could feel himself shaking. He'd been hoping all the booby traps had been deactivated. The animated dragon's roaring appeared to be responsible for the roof collapsing but he couldn't be sure. He wondered if it was a trick and if he dared take the risk.

"Well hero? The clock's ticking. Will you give me the fascinating costume or do I kill your little friends and take it. Just to show you I am serious, watch this."

The Dragon pushed another button on his gauntlet. The countdown accelerated and his animated counterpart roared. Then he calmly pushed another button on his other gauntlet and metal spikes emerged on his gloved fingertips. Before The Guardian could react, he stabbed the slowly stirring Bat Boy.

Will and Alex started struggling frantically against their chains, their terrified cries for help becoming increasingly desperate.

The Dragon knelt down, checking Bat Boy's neck for a pulse. He shrugged and stood up.

The Guardian knew his time was up. He had only one option. He attacked. Swinging as he came, he charged The Dragon but The Dragon calmly caught his fist in midair and squeezed. The Guardian was forced to his knees.

"Never make business this personal. Don't lose your head. You'll always come off worse in the deal," The Dragon said calmly as his other hand reached for The Guardian's throat.

The mercenary smiled triumphantly. The Guardian could see the pleasure in The Dragon's eyes as he punished the upstart brat who had ruined his easy business deal. The Guardian felt a blow to his ribs for good measure as the dragon smiled still more broadly. Unfortunately for the arsonist, he couldn't see The Guardian's own grin.

"You know I don't like Cane Toads. Their defence isn't subtle. They poison everything. I prefer sea snakes because they're peaceful. They don't bite until you grab or provoke them," The Guardian said conversationally between gasps for breath.

He produced the knife he'd taken from The Dragon's other henchman. With all the speed he could muster he stabbed the control panel on The Dragon's gauntlet.

There was a blinding white flash and a stabbing pain went through The Guardian's body as he heard a tremendous bang. For a few seconds, he flew through the air. He would have smashed into the big screen TV but the realization that he was flying caused his costume to activate the anti-gravity feature. Instead he merely floated in front of the screen which he realized had caught fire. The Dragon wasn't so lucky. He laid in a crumpled heap, sparks coming from his gauntlet.

The Guardian knew it was time to go. Flames were rapidly spreading from the ruined television. The Guardian wasn't sure how the TV was rigged to explode but even if he'd succeeded in deactivating The Dragon's ability to detonate the bomb, eventually the fire would reach the explosives or The Dragon's jet pack. The warehouse would soon be blown sky high.

The Guardian ran. Will was closer to The Dragon and the immediate danger posed by the jet pack. Will and Alex looked at The Guardian with wide eyes. They no longer struggled or called for help. They hung limply in their chains, clearly beyond hope.

The Guardian reached Will and broke his chains with ease.

Putting his arm over Will's shoulder, The Guardian helped him to his feet. Out of the corner of his eye he saw a stack of crates sway dangerously.

He grabbed Will and jumped. The stack fell. The crates smashed and shards of debris flew over the boys' heads.

Will had a small cut on one cheek but was otherwise unharmed. The Guardian thought he heard faint footsteps.

The Guardian didn't have time to look around or worry. Wishing he had the strength to carry Alex too, he headed for the nearest window.

"What exactly are you going to do?" Will demanded.

"Fly. Don't worry, I've done it safely once," The Guardian said.

Will had the same appalled expression on his face he'd had when Kevin had suggested asking if they could go mountain climbing as part of Kevin's grand plan to conquer his fear of heights. The Guardian decided it would be best if Will didn't have time to think about this anymore. He jumped.

The Guardian flew. Will was screaming and hanging on so tight that he had The Guardian in a stranglehold. The Guardian really wished people would stop doing that. He was relieved when Will's screaming stopped; at least for a few seconds.

"Look out!" Will shouted.

The Guardian looked behind him. Something was flying towards them as they reached the ground. The Guardian realized it was The Dragon's jet pack with the ruined gantlet attached to it. They landed, in front of the parking garage where The Guardian had tied up The Dragon's guards.

Even though he had no idea if his suit could save them from the explosion and knowing that he didn't have the size difference to adequately shield his best friend, The Guardian knelt over Will, hoping to protect him the way he'd shielded Carol.

The jet pack exploded above their heads. Amazingly both boys saw a force field of blue energy surround them in a protective bobble.

"Cool I didn't know I could do that! The Guardian said happily.

"You mean you saved us by a fluke or hunch!" Will said in outrage.

"Yeah, let's go with hunch," The Guardian replied trying to sound as confident as possible.

The Guardian took off, flying towards the window before Will could interrogate him further. He had a funny feeling this was getting into dangerous territory. Sure enough, as he landed in the warehouse he could hear Will yelling.

"Do I know you?"

The Guardian looked around. The smoke and flame now filled the warehouse. Luckily the flames hadn't reached Alex. The Guardian still heard him coughing and struggling against his chains.

He'd almost made it to Alex when somebody punched The Guardian in the side of the head.

"Still here mate. Last chance. Do I use fire to create or destroy?" The Dragon snarled.

The Guardian figured this was a rhetorical question. The Dragon didn't look like he was in the mood to make deals. His face was covered in soot and blood, and one of his goggles was smashed, the now exposed eye gleaming murderously.

The Guardian used all his super powered strength to shove The Dragon away from him. The Dragon sailed across the room, crashing into a pillar. The Guardian knew he didn't have much time. He flew across the warehouse towards Alex, flying as high as he could to avoid the smoke. Just as he reached Alex, the beam below The Guardian caught fire. Looking down he saw The Dragon smiling vindictively with his palm aimed straight at The Guardian.

Suddenly they both heard a thunderous crack. The Dragon's triumphant smile vanished. He looked up in surprise at the large beam falling towards his head. He tried to run but tripped and an instant later the beam landed on him, pinning his legs to the ground.

The Guardian turned around, heading for The Dragon but then he stopped in his tracks. He knew he didn't have time to save them both before the building burned down.

"Help me! I am the only one who can prove who hired me. It was nothing personal mate, just business. You've seen the way Sheila does business. Imagine all the people you can save!" The Dragon shouted desperately.

"A dragon's treasure is always cursed, and stop calling me mate."

The Guardian walked calmly over to Alex, snapped his chains and tossed the bomb away from them, thinking he would come back for the mercenary.

He scooped the now barely conscious Alex into his arms and carried him to the window. He'd just taken off, when he heard The Dragon's voice.

"I know who you are hero!"

The Guardian touched down safely and without a sound at the parking garage where he'd left Will. The Dragon's henchmen were still there tied up out of harm's way. When he put Alex down, The Guardian was amazed to see he was grinning from ear to ear.

"That was awesome! We got abducted by aliens and rescued by a superhero!" he said, clapping a stunned Will's shoulder.

The Guardian couldn't help laughing as Will and Alex started arguing. They continued even as police cars, a fire truck and an ambulance, and of course news vans showed up on the other side of the street. The Guardian turned away from his friends, knowing there was still one more person he needed to rescue. He was heading back towards the warehouse just as it exploded, collapsing into rubble.

• • • • • • • • • •

TWO DAYS LATER...

No matter where you went in Braxton; the school, the shopping center, the retirement home or the swimming pool there was only one topic of conversation. The newest urban legend to appear in this city that had been filled with urban legends for twenty years ever since people had seen strange lights in the sky one summer night. This latest urban legend was about The Guardian.

Like all urban legends, the details of the story varied depending on who was telling it. This was a young urban legend so most versions had several basic elements. No matter how outlandish the tale, the basic legend was the same.

Three teenagers claimed they had been kidnapped. They couldn't agree whether it was by an alien, a mutant or a lunatic in a mask. They did agree that The Guardian had fought the kidnapper, who later killed himself in a fire.

Of course, residents argued over what this meant. Some said the whole story was a hoax; others believed the aliens had come back for a visit. One of the teenagers was a fan of this theory. Most people simply decided the teenagers were drunk, delusional or on drugs.

The problems with these explanations were that there really was a fire and explosion. Wanted criminals were found hogtied near the fire and the same criminals had been broken out of jail hours later. Everyone was once again wondering where The Guardian was now.

Helen Montgomery looked up from making cookies. She smiled as she continued to calmly knead the chocolate chip cookie dough. She held some out as The Guardian dropped through the cafeteria window.

"I've wanted to meet you for some time. You've made quite a name for yourself. I don't think Braxton will be able to pretend recent events never happened thanks to certain reporters and websites," Helen said calmly.

The Guardian couldn't believe how relaxed Helen Montgomery was. She picked up her rolling pin to start flattening her dough.

"I know you are behind the fires and the disappearance of Nigel Hawthorne," The Guardian said.

Helen Montgomery walked to the oven. She opened the oven, putting in her latest batch of cookies.

"Who is Nigel Hawthorne?" She asked frowning.

"Play dumb all you want. I sent all the evidence to the cops," The Guardian replied.

Helen Montgomery shrugged. She walked over to a drawer and started rummaging inside. The Guardian turned to leave but she tossed something on the counter with unnecessary force, stopping him in his tracks.

"You know the key to the perfect cookie is making sure you have all the ingredients," Helen Montgomery said pointing to the counter.

The Guardian zoomed in on the counter with his visor. He saw a CD case on top of a yellow file folder. The folder had the word evidence stamped across it and The Guardian recognized his father's handwriting.

"I don't like cookies. I prefer games. Never start a game until you know the rules. I know you think you own Braxton but I will be watching you," The Guardian said and vanished before Helen could stop him.

Kevin Rigby sat on his bed scratching Merlin behind the ears. Two weeks ago, he'd been an ordinary teenager. Now he was a superhero complete with an arch enemy. Helen Montgomery was powerful but Kevin would stop her eventually. For now, he was going to learn to bounce the Moon. He picked up the phone.

"Hi, it's Kevin. Is Will home?

CPSIA information can be obtained
at www.ICGtesting.com
Printed in the USA
LVHW091628310121
677957LV00025B/1145

9 781525 501203